Silent Rage

DE Funk

Silent Rage

DE Funk

Editor: Linda Gilden
www.lindagilden.com

Cover design: Patti Rishforth
www.heartpaperscissors.com

Cover image: Merideth Funk

First Printing, 2018

ISBN 9781728758923

Kindle Direct Publishing
www.kdp.amazon.com

Printed in the United States of America

Dedication

To my parents

Acknowledgements

I would like to thank my family for believing in me and encouraging me as I tackled this new endeavor. Their support means everything to me and I could not have accomplished it without them. A special thank you to my husband, Chris, who listened to multiple readings of the book as I worked on it as well as set-up my website. Katy gets a special shout out along with my thanks for coordinating the social media world for me. Meri gave me some great ideas as well as took some amazing photos. I could not have accomplished anything without the prayerful support of Ronnie. He always checked on my progress and provided me with lots of encouragement. I'd also like to thank Kris Wampler for giving me invaluable legal advice and for simply listening to my ideas. Good luck to Kris with his writing career.

My sincere thanks go to my fantastic editor, Linda Gilden, who truly pulled a better book out of me. Her advice and guidance on getting me ready to launch my first novel proved invaluable. She has tirelessly worked to get me ready for a much wider audience. I am eternally grateful for all her tutelage.

Acknowledgements

Silent Rage is a work of fiction, however, at the core of it is a young man who had a lot of issues to overcome. I believe many juvenile delinquents would never have that label applied to them if the proper mental health interventions were available. Middle school is a challenging time for adolescents and if schools incorporated a curriculum which included courses in dealing with such issues as anger, bullying, and peer pressure, to name a few there, would potentially be less juvenile crime. This would also carry over into adulthood. I've worked with troubled kids and have seen them try and tackle adult issues. It is never an easy thing for them. If you know a troubled youth, reach out and help.

Silent Rage

Chapter 1
Russell

The woods were dark that night, only gaining light from the half-moon when the clouds opened up to reveal the orb. Spanish moss that draped the limbs of the oaks danced an eerie sort of pirate jig which was appropriate for these prisoners. The men were captives of the infamous Edward Teach, more commonly known as Blackbeard. He caught the old dogs stealing some of his cargo. Teach had recently commandeered a shipment of some chests of indigo and planned to make a hefty profit from the sale of the blue dye but the unfortunate sailors tried to beat him to the cash by selling the plunder locally. No one stole from Blackbeard and lived to tell about it.

To punish the sailors for their disloyalty, Blackbeard had imposed a penalty on them he learned about from rumors of things an older and equally notorious pirate did to his victims. It was called woolding and involved placing a leather strap around the person's head and then using a metal rod to tighten the strap in such a way that ultimately the pressure would cause the victim's eyes to pop out. Blackbeard simply kicked the discarded eyeballs out of his way often squishing one of them. After the torture, Blackbeard had the dead men's bodies hung from the trees nearby to warn anyone what fate awaited them should they try and steal any of his bootie. The corpses were his gift to the southern lands that had richly provided him chests of blue gold.

Blackbeard didn't discriminate between men and women in his business dealings. In fact, he preferred the ladies and always put pleasure before business with the females. He left a lot of broken hearts in his wake and rumor has it, a few offspring. Over 300 years later anyone living along the southern coast with the surname of Teach claimed they descended from the infamous buccaneer.

The pirates were long gone and now a young boy stood in the same woods where Blackbeard once roamed. The youth figured the swashbuckler wouldn't mind the use of the old oak trees for a different purpose. The boy didn't plan to hang anyone from the thick and low-growing branches of the trees, but he was leaving a bounty of sorts. It would be a veritable feast for the trees and insects who dwelled there. The boy gazed at the gnarly limbs of the trees and he liked that they were now the guardians of his bootie. He thought Edward Teach would approve.

The boy had a teacher named Miss Teach. He wondered if she was related to Blackbeard. He didn't think so because she was nice and real pretty with long blonde hair. She didn't look like a pirate at all. The boy quit his musings about the pirates and turned his attention back to his task. It was hot and the cicada bugs had ceased their infernal and loud chirping. The boy hadn't noticed the silence until he had finished with his cutting. The bugs could be so loud they drowned out all other noise in the vicinity. At the moment, however, it was eerily quiet. All of the animals and insects had ceased any noise making. It was as if none of them wanted anyone else to come and invade their territory. As a matter of fact, they were waiting for the human to leave so they could begin attacking the feast that was spread out below them. Soon the woods would be alive with all of the party goers. Even now the first of hundreds of flies were enroute to make their presence known to the other attendees. They would do the most damage to the meal.

Over 100,000 different species of flies exist. The most popular is the blowfly. It's the first to arrive on the scene of a crime where there's blood and a dead body. The wings of the pest are attached to types of hinges that allow the insect to move its wings about a hundred times a second. Scientists have tried to study just how fast a blowfly can fly but no one has arrived at a definitive answer. The first blowflies to arrive on the scene of a fresh carcass do so within minutes of the deceased's last breath. Just like the cicada bug made its own noise, so too do a swarm of flies when they feast on a dead body. The killer knew these facts about the blowfly because he had read them in a science book at the library. He was fascinated with entomology. So when he saw a fly buzz past his head he knew the first place it would land would be on the blood that pooled around his victim's body. He knew it would be the first of masses of the invasive insects to come. The flies would be a variety of color, among them blue, green, or black.

The woman was not bothered by the insects swarming around her. She didn't even swat at any of them. She couldn't. She just lay there with her mouth hanging open. It looked like she was almost trying to grin. That was impossible now. As a matter of fact, she wasn't capable of ever smiling again, she never did anyway. No one was going to miss her. She was an old woman and had no family. Later forensics would reveal she had been stabbed in the chest 17 times, in the stomach 15 times, and in her genital region 5 times. The fatal wound reached deep into her heart basically cutting it in half. She did not die easily.

Her killer stared at her in fascination. He liked that a fly had already landed on her because he knew she would soon be crawling in maggots. He read once that a swarm of maggots could eat forty pounds of flesh in a day. He hoped it wouldn't take long for her to decay and become a part of the earth. He couldn't stand the old woman who was the counselor from his school. Now she'd really be out of his life forever. He wiped the blade with the rag he brought for just that purpose. He thought to himself – *a good soldier always cleans his weapons.*

He dragged her body deeper into the woods and left her for the animals to enjoy. *Maybe they would like her cause no one else did.* The killer turned around and left the old woman. No one would miss her for several days. No one would find her for over a decade. No one knew it was his first kill. He was thirteen.

Chapter 2
Roger Allen Watson

The prison had placed Roger Allen Watson under a deathwatch. But to him that was a joke and waste of time for the guard. He wasn't about to kill himself. He wanted someone else to look him in the eyes while his life ebbed away and feel the power it gave to a person who took the life of another. Maybe his death would inspire someone else to hunt down a victim and take his life. That way even in his execution Roger Watson would've given birth to a killer legacy.

The hours before his demise passed quickly and without any major problems. On the day of the execution condemned prisoners are allowed many visitors. Roger had none. He was allowed two phone calls but he had no one he wanted to say goodbye to. He sat alone for his last meal which consisted of a hamburger, fries, and a chocolate shake. He was allowed to enjoy a nice long, hot shower after which he was given a new pair of pants and shirt to put on for the big moment. When the hour came to be escorted to the execution chamber, he wanted no minister or spiritual advisor to walk with him chanting meaningless platitudes. Meaningless to him anyway.

"It's time." The big, burly guard rapped on the door to Roger's cell. Roger turned his back to the guard and shuffled backward to the door so the handcuffs could be placed around his wrists. He was glad this was the final time he felt the metal bracelets around him. The cell door opened and Roger was accompanied by the warden and three guards to the death room.

Silent Rage

They reached the ridiculously cheerful room, painted a bright shade of sunshine and adorned with custom made plaid draperies for the viewing window. They were currently closed but would be pulled open once Roger was strapped in the bed.

"Get on up there," the big guard told Roger. There was a small stepstool to make the climb onto the tall fixture easier for the person about to die. Roger stepped on it and then laid down for his final night's sleep in the prison. He had heard horror stories about botched executions. He hoped his went fast. He was ready to get to hell and make some ruckus there. He didn't believe in Heaven but he did believe there was a place for people like him to try and outdo each other. He was ready for the freedom from this place.

Roger put his head on the pillow and stretched out his arms on the two paddle-like extensions on the bed to make the veins easier to get to for the death team. Six straps were placed around his body. Roger took a deep breath and swallowed. He could feel his heart racing. He did not like being penned down. The team continued to prep him for the big event. Once he was ready, they repositioned the bed which put him in a semblance of a standing position allowing him to face the window and the occupants gathered on the other side. The curtains were pulled back and the audience gave a collective gasp.

"Do you have any last words you would like to say to your victims' families?" Warden Gray asked Roger.

Roger's soulless eyes looked out at the family representatives of some of the girls he had killed. Of course, not every girl he killed had someone there to watch his demise. There were more victims who were yet to be discovered and linked to him. *I'll never tell now*, he thought to himself. He knew he was expected to share his feelings of remorse but he just couldn't bring himself to say the words the audience wanted to hear. Besides, he wasn't sorry. He had enjoyed his career.

"I would like to tell the families thank you for giving me such fine young women to enjoy." This comment brought another gasp from the audience and this time the gasp was not in pity but in horror. One dad stood and ran to the window and banged on it. "I hope you rot in hell and feel your everlasting torture for eternity." A guard gently took the overwrought father by the shoulders and escorted him back to his seat.

The warden nodded to the guard to lower the death bed and begin the process of the death sentence. The Execution Team, which consisted of five medical professionals, stepped forward to start the execution. Roger was given an anesthetic which would lull him into a peaceful rest. Supposedly he would never feel a thing. Next he would be administered a muscle relaxer. Finally, the last mixture of the lethal cocktail would be pumped into his veins and his heart would simply stop.

The execution of Roger Allen Watson did not go swiftly or easily. What actually happened was a horrid death. Some of the observers would never forget what they saw that day while others would feel a sort of justice that at the end Roger got what he deserved. When the drugs entered his system, Roger's body convulsed and shook for 12 minutes before he sighed his last breath. In the process he bit his tongue and his fingernails cut eight half-moons into his palms. He wet himself and his bowels released filling the small room with a horrific stench.

Silent Rage

When it was all over the drapes were pulled closed, the discarded needles and syringes were trashed, and the body of the notorious Trailer Park Murderer was carted to the morgue where a state ordered autopsy would be performed. Most States still required the body of an executed person to be autopsied because it was not a natural death. Ironically, on the executed criminal's death certificate the cause of death would be listed as homicide. Not that any sense of justice for the families of the victims would be gained from the examination but there was always the possibility some sort of disease would be uncovered that would explain why the person killed.

The infamous murderer of young girls was executed for the heinous mutilation of several girls, one of whom was a pretty and popular sophomore. The blond haired and blue-eyed Melissa Templeton had been a high school cheerleader and homecoming queen who had caught the attention of a nation when she went missing. She was found a week later by some hikers on a path near a popular picnic area. They smelled something foul and left the trail to investigate. They had read the newspapers and heard the television reports about a missing girl and they thought "what if?" Their suspicions proved correct and they found the body of young Melissa not far from the trailer park she called home.

Melissa's corpse clearly revealed a gruesome death when the autopsy report was finished. She had been raped, stabbed, beaten and ultimately strangled to death. The country wanted justice. With the arrest and conviction of Roger everyone thought they had achieved it. No one would know for years that Roger had left behind more than victims. Everyone thought his impact died with him. How wrong they were. But the nightmare that was The Trailer Park Murderer was over and when the news reported the conclusion of the execution there were cheers around the country. The words of the warden giving a false sense of finality.

"At 12:14 a.m. Roger Allen Watson was officially pronounced dead. Thank you." Warden Gray left the podium amidst cheers, angry shouts, and questions from the media. Most of the world was happy the killer was dead but there were the usual protestors, who only thought about the criminal, demanding an end to the cruel and unusual punishment of the death penalty. Gray was not going to get into a debate on the ethics of the death penalty. He simply did his job. In his opinion this criminal deserved much worse for what he did to his victims. Didn't anybody ever think about them?

Chapter 3
Loretta

Loretta Thomas turned off the television. She didn't want to hear any more about the father of her child. She knew the man a long time ago and he didn't even know he had a kid with her. Roger was a creep who raped her when she was fourteen. Her mind drifted back to the summer before high school.

It was 1992 and Vanessa Williams's number one song was playing in Loretta's head. *Yep,* she thought, *he saved the best for last with me.* A good looking guy had tried to hit on several girls at the local diner but when he saw Loretta he moved straight toward her as if no one else was in the room. It was just like in a movie, at least in Loretta's mind it was. He sweet talked her into going out with him and once in his car he drove down a dirt road and parked the vehicle.

Then her nightmare began. To say he beat her would be putting it mildly. He savagely kicked her, punched her, stabbed her with his pocketknife which fortunately wasn't very long, and then when she was practically unconscious he stripped her naked and began to bite her in places she never told a soul about. He rammed his penis into her without any attempt at being gentle to the young virgin and poured himself into her. When it was over he got in his car and drove off never checking to see if she was alive or dead. He hoped she was dead. Then he could say he'd done it with a corpse. He would like that. Loretta laid on that dirt road for at least an hour before getting up and beginning the walk home. It turned out she was only about a mile from her mobile home park. It was a long and painful mile to walk. Plus, it was dark and she was afraid he would come back to finish the job of killing her. She had no doubt that was his intention. He was a violent and evil man.

When she got home after her so called date, her mother took one look at her and said: "Well, I guess you done burst your cherry and got beat up for it. If you get knocked up, you can get your sorry ass out of my home. I ain't paying for no brat from some loser." Nine months later and just after her fifteenth birthday, Loretta left home and never saw her mother again.

It had been over a decade since that night and Loretta had done all she could to make a life for herself and her son. It wasn't easy. She didn't have any skills other than showing off the figure she was blessed with. It was a good one. Men parted with their hard earned dollars by sticking them in all sorts of places on her skimpy costumes. She gyrated and moved and shook her double D's in their faces all for a cheap thrill. For an extra fee she would take an eager patron into a back room and let him have a feel of her natural size D breasts. If he wanted to go further more money had to exchange hands first. Her breasts were her best feature and made her decent money but she was also pretty good at turning tricks for the club owner. Currently she was his star employee. A man she knew only as Lucky Sam.

Years ago he happened to see the young beauty offering blowjobs for cash. Lucky Sam knew a good money maker when he saw one so he offered the girl a place to stay in exchange for a job. The fact she was pregnant was ok with him because it would just keep her obligated to him. He found her a mobile home, which she still lives in today, and let her keep her baby as long as she took care of things for him and made him money. Loretta became very good at her job. Lucky Sam was pleased and considered himself pretty damn lucky to have stumbled across her that night. Loretta was his solid gold good luck charm.

Loretta peaked into the room of her sleeping son and was very glad to have someone to love and who loved her back. So what if his daddy was a serial killer who murdered at least two young women before his so called date with Loretta. Her son would never know that. His birth certificate said "father unknown."

She had known Roger was someone who had been in trouble with the law back then, but he was just so good looking she couldn't believe he was really all that bad. As a young teenager she thought for sure the police were wrong. They picked on people from her neighborhood anyway. Today, however, she knew the night she met him he had just been released from prison and was also wanted for questioning in the "Trailer Park Murders." Loretta knew she was lucky to have escaped him that night. The fact he had knocked her unconscious actually saved her life. Plus, he had not had time to get him a new kabar knife, which was his go-to blade for killing young girls. When he finished with Loretta he thought she was dead or at least close to it.

Anxious to go get a drink, Roger simply left Loretta on that old dirt road and figured the buzzards would take care of her. Had Loretta gone to the police she would have saved the lives of five more girls. But she didn't know that. After all she was only fourteen when it happened. How was she supposed to know he was going to keep on killing?

When he was finally arrested he pled guilty and waived all appeals. His court-appointed lawyer did his best to postpone the execution but in the end it was what Roger wanted as well as the public. He was a sadistic killer who enjoyed torturing his victims before, during, and after his violent rape of them. No one was really sorry he was gone. The only people protesting his execution were the same ones who protested every execution because they didn't support capital punishment. Loretta would've been happy to be the one to stick the needle in his arm. *Good riddance,* she thought.

Loretta made her way to her kitchen sink where she washed the dishes that were piling up. She stared out of the small, dirty window and thought about her past. How had she ended up in this godforsaken mobile home? Just outside in the street by her place a small group of derelicts was hanging out and leaning against her car. Loretta squinted to see who was there. She knew they were up to no good. As a matter of fact, she had even bought some drugs from them herself. That was a last resort for her, though. Usually she could get what she wanted at the club where she worked. But lately her boss was watching her and had been on her case about the amount of drugs she was using. She needed to keep him happy since he was the one who stepped in and helped her when she had needed it most. She truly wanted to get cleaned up but the cravings were getting harder and harder to ignore and, frankly, her life was so pitiful the drugs helped her escape. She got back to her washing and ignored the guys outside.

The miscreants hanging around Loretta's trailer were indeed up to no good. They were swapping drugs and money and discussing new ways to get high.

"You gonna get us something different, man? I'm tired of the same shitty high." Leo was a pimply faced kid of about nineteen who was clearly addicted to meth given his complexion and gray teeth.

"I got something comin'. Probably have it after my shift at Sassy A." Bud was the local go to guy for most drugs. Users like Leo were always looking for a new way to get high and forget about their miserable existence. Ironically, Bud was a conscientious drug dealer. He didn't want his regulars getting messed up and dying. But he was afraid his supplier was going to make him start pushing more heroin and meth. If these guys mixed the drugs they'd for sure get the high they wanted because this concoction was called a speedball and was often lethal. He was afraid it'd also be their last time trying it. That kind of drug just sounded messed up. Bud, however, liked his lifestyle and had all he needed. It was important to keep his customers supplied, happy, and preferably not dead. He might have serious concerns for his customers but in the end he'd still wind up selling to them. "You gonna take this or not?" Bud asked Leo handing him his daily fix.

"I want it. I'm just looking for maybe a better high, know what I mean?" Leo forked over the cash he had to cover his day's hit.

Bud pocketed the money and moved on to the next guy, dismissing Leo. By the end of his session Bud had well over a thousand dollars in his pocket and about half of that was his. All for a measly thirty minutes of work. Not a bad return. *Sure beats washing dishes,* thought Bud. Bud's other job was washing dishes at the Sassy A which was also the home of his supplier. No one knew that though, and Bud wasn't telling. Snitches didn't last long in his neck of the woods.

Chapter 4
Libby

Across town in a more upscale neighborhood, one that was free from the dangers of the drug trade, Libby Teach watched the news and saw the execution. She felt only relief that Roger Allen Watson was dead. Her secret would now be buried forever. Uncle Roger was a terrible man who had molested her when she was nine years old. He convinced her not to tell anyone because she would get in trouble. He told her no one believed kids anyway. Uncle Roger was actually Libby's mother's uncle. He was a surprise to his parents and was born in their twilight years so he was ridiculously spoiled.

A good looking guy who always got what he wanted, Roger seemed to have no moral compass when it came to girls. He liked them all and age was just a number to him. Whenever he visited Libby's family he was on his best behavior so that he could enjoy the delicious meals and comfortable bed that Libby's mother provided for him. Roger was always careful to treat Libby with the right amount of attention any child would receive from a loving uncle. Then one day when Libby was playing in the sprinklers in her yard, Roger appeared out of nowhere and just stared at Libby. When Libby asked him what he wanted, he invited her to go with him to get some ice cream. Since that was her favorite treat she quickly agreed. Libby threw on a cover-up and the two went off for ice cream.

That was the day Roger molested her. It started very innocently when he began wiping off some of the cold treat from her cover up.

16

The two went out to get in his burgundy 1981 Honda Accord. Roger helped Libby get in the passenger side of the car and even reached in to buckle her in the seat belt.

"I love ice cream! Especially when it's with my favorite Libby Gal." Roger always called her Libby Gal. After the ice cream incident, she hated that name.

"I like chocolate best." Libby said.

"I like any flavor as long as I'm with my best gal."

They drove the short distant to a local ice cream parlor. When they opened the door they were treated to a rush of cold air as well as an assortment of sweet scented aromas. The teenaged girl standing behind the counter took one look at the good-looking man and immediately went to stand in front of him.

"What can I get you?" the girl asked. She was an average looking girl of average size and average brown hair. She did not make an impression on Roger who was giving Libby all of his attention.

"Libby Gal, how about if we both get a double scoop of chocolate on a sugar cone?" Roger asked Libby.

"Yes, I'd like that."

"Well you heard the girl, get us each a double scoop of chocolate and go heavy on the scoop." Roger winked to the girl as he said it. Not because he thought the girl was pretty but simply because his experience with females taught him a little bit of flirting went a long way in getting him what he wanted. It worked on anything from an ice cream scoop to sex. Roger knew how to use his good looks to his advantage.

"Here you go and that'll be eight bucks, please." The clerk handed the two cones to Roger. Roger took them and gave Libby one as he took a big lick of his ice cream.

"Mmmmm, delicious." Roger handed the clerk a ten-dollar bill and waited for his change.

"Thanks and come back any time," the girl said as Roger and Libby turned to leave but Roger had already forgotten the girl was there.

"Let's go eat these in the booth in that corner back there." Roger pointed to a booth situated in the back of the store and behind a structural pole. It gave an illusion of privacy for the occupants of the booth. "How's yours, Libby Gal?"

"It's good. Cold too. I had brain freeze for a second."

"Aw I hate when that happens."

Both of them took a moment to nibble at their cold desserts in silence. Libby's treat was melting faster than she could consume it.

"Libby Gal, you dripped some chocolate on your pool dress." Roger was enjoying watching Libby's small pink tongue lick at the ice cream. He imagined what it would feel like on his skin. He had discovered he liked young girls and he started to get excited just thinking about that soft tongue licking him wherever he directed. *Damn, I want a piece of that,* he thought. He decided he deserved something from her since he took her to get the ice cream. Libby was already a pretty girl and was just beginning to blossom into a woman. Roger liked little girls. He could have just left her alone but she looked so innocent he knew he wanted to try and get her to himself. He got out of his seat and went to sit beside her.

18

"Here, let me wipe that off for you." He grabbed several napkins from the silver dispenser located on the table and started smearing the chocolate further down the front of her cover up.

"Uncle Roger, you're making it worse. Let me do it." Libby tried to grab the napkins from him but he wouldn't let her.

"I am happy to help my favorite niece." Roger continued moving his hand up and down the front of the bathing suit cover up. He was enjoying the feel of the small buds that were just forming in route to making Libby become a woman.

"Uncle Roger, stop it. I can do it and you've made it worse."

Roger was caught up his perverse enjoyment and ignored Libby. He continued rubbing her chest and increased his pressure. Libby was scared and had never seen her uncle like this. She screamed and ran to the bathroom, dropping her cone on the floor as she escaped.

"Libby Gal, come back." Roger called after her but she had already gone into the ladies' room.

The clerk who had served them the ice cream walked over to see if she could help.

"Everything's ok. She just dropped her ice cream." Roger said.

"Poor girl. I can get her another if you think she wants more." The clerk was trying to gain some favorable attention from the good looking customer.

"No, we've got to leave." The clerk watched as Roger got up and walked to the bathroom and gave a rap on the door.

"Libby Gal? It's ok. Come on out and I'll take you back home."

Libby was inside frantically wiping the chocolate stain and making no progress with it. The cover-up was ruined and she wanted to get away from Uncle Roger. She knew he shouldn't have tried to help her. There was something wrong about the way he was wiping off the chocolate. Libby decided she had to get home and away from Uncle Roger but knew she had to endure the ride back home with him.

Libby opened up the door and rushed past Roger. "Just take me home now."

"No problem. Let's go." The two went out and got in the car. This time Roger did not help Libby with her seat belt. He started the car and began the drive back. Roger was still mad he didn't get to have a little more of Libby. He noticed a dirt road up ahead and turned down it.

Libby saw the street go by and knew this wasn't the way home. "Where are we going?"

"I want to talk and can do it better when I'm not focused on driving," Roger said.

"I want to go home. I'm cold and my cover-up is wet."

Roger pulled the car over and parked. He turned to Libby and put his hand along the seat behind Libby and squeezed her shoulder. "Libby Gal, you never told me thank you for the ice cream, and a lady always thanks a gentleman when he treats her to something."

"Oh, well thanks. Now let's go home." Libby had yet to look at Roger.

"Libby Gal, I want you to turn and look at me and let me know how much you enjoyed the treat."

Libby looked sideways at Roger and murmured a thanks again. Roger was getting irritated with her now.

"That's not good enough. Look at me." He grabbed her face and turned it to him and then he kissed her roughly. He used his free hand to put it between her legs and tugged at her bathing suit.

"Stop it!" Libby was scared and was trying to push her uncle away. Roger was caught up in his own world and didn't care about Libby's struggles. Instead he was getting more aroused with her fighting.

"I said stop it. This isn't right." Libby said each word with a struggle and managed to get one hand on his face and scratched him deeply. Roger reacted by putting his hand on his face and feeling it moist with blood.

"You little bitch. So you like it rough, do ya?" Roger still held onto Libby with one hand. He didn't want the girl to go and tell anyone and get him in trouble with the law. People would know he was the last one with her and he wasn't about to go back to prison. He knew she was upset but didn't want her telling anyone what had happened. "Libby Gal, tell you what. Let's just forget about this and I'll take you home now. But if you tell anyone what happened I'm going to be mad and you don't want to see me mad."

"I won't tell," Libby said. She refused to look at him and gazed out of the window still struggling to get her arm free.

"I'm serious. If you tell anyone not only will I be mad at you but I will come after you and knock some sense into you. I will also take that stupid dog you love and gut him and leave him in the woods for the bears to eat."

Silent Rage

"You leave my dog alone!" Libby was upset and looked at her uncle and this time didn't see a favorite relative but rather a crazy and evil man. She was scared and rightly so. "I won't tell." At this point Libby managed to get her arm free and opened the car door opened. As she got out Roger grabbed one of her legs and tried to drag her back. She kicked herself free and took off running in the direction of home as she heard Roger drive away. Her home was not far from the dirt road and she ran all the way and straight to her bedroom. Locking the door behind her she stripped off the offending cover-up and buried it deep in the trashcan in her room.

Roger never came back to the house after that day and eventually his bad ways caught up with him. He ended up going to prison on multiple occasions. Ultimately he was arrested for murder which ended with his death by lethal injection. Libby never told anyone about that day and she still couldn't eat chocolate ice cream.

Libby shuddered at the memory of the vile man. She switched channels to a sappy love story and got on with grading the test papers from her sixth grade history class. She was determined to put Uncle Roger out of her mind forever. Eventually the papers were all corrected and the scores were logged into the computer. Libby got ready for bed and planned to read herself to sleep.

Chapter 5
Russell

"Hey Punk! Clean up this pig sty!" Those words hurled from the shiny fat lips of Wayne Jetsoe, whom Russell secretly called Fatso, his mom's lover. Russell hated those lips because they did evil things to his private parts and then told him to do the same evil things back. One day Russell was going to peel those lips right off that hideous face.

Wayne sat on the stained and torn sofa in the doublewide mobile home where he and his mom lived. The place was a mess and stank of old pizza. His mom was not a very good housekeeper. Of course the pig sty was mostly a result of Wayne's abandoned empty beer cans. Since it was a hot, early fall day the flies were out in full force in the small room and were swarming around Wayne. The flies were having a feast with the crumbs stuck in Wayne's scraggly beard and he expected 12-year-old Russell to take care of the problem.

Russell hated Wayne and sure didn't see him as any kind of father figure even if his mom did refer to him as dad when Russell was around. Russell had no idea who his real father was and his mom, Loretta, wouldn't ever talk about him. She had gotten pregnant at the age of 14 and her own mom threw her out of the house forcing Loretta to do whatever she could to survive. Loretta loved Russell but she just never had a chance herself and often looked the other way when things didn't go like she wanted. Recently, Loretta had gotten hooked on heroin and was forced to put up with the likes of Wayne just to support her habit.

Silent Rage

At the age of 27 soon to be 28, Loretta was still a looker and had a slim yet full-busted figure which served her well at her job as a stripper. She earned a decent amount of money but more and more of it was going to support her drug habit. Russell had already been forced to call 911 on his mom twice for overdoses. It was simply a matter of time before he was an orphan.

Russell often had to be the man of the house which made him live in a grown up world. All he really wanted was to hunt and ride his bike and maybe get a dog. His sixth grade class had watched a classic movie called Old Yeller about a boy and his dog and ever since then Russell wanted to get one himself. In reality, he probably wouldn't have been a good pet owner because he typically kicked little animals when he saw them. It was his way of beating up on something smaller than himself since he was usually the one getting kicked around. Russell was small for his age and his mom had even held Russell back and made him repeat kindergarten. The other kids in his class were aware of this so Wayne wasn't the only person who bullied him. Classmates were always taunting Russell and calling him names like "pipsqueak" and "no muscle Russell" and even "retard" but he had plans to show them all someday just how strong he was.

"Punk!" Wayne's fist accompanied his yelling this time and he hit Russell on the head so hard it literally caused him to fall down. Picking himself up and holding his hand to his ear, Russell forgot all thoughts of a dog and instead focused his attention on how to get back at Wayne for always hitting him. This was getting to be all too common and even Loretta seemed to care more about getting her daily fix than she did his frequent beatings.

Silent Rage

Last night after Russell fell asleep, his mom and Wayne got wasted on booze and drugs. Evidently the party didn't end for his mom because she was strung out on the couch and barely aware of anything. These were the times Wayne was the meanest. When Wayne hit Russell, Loretta didn't even put up any kind of argument to stop him. She simply closed her eyes. Russell felt betrayed as if she loved the drugs more than him. He loved his mother but when she was high he hated her because she didn't stop the bad things from happening.

Russell cleaned up as well as any twelve-year-old, soon to be thirteen, could and then escaped to his secret hideaway. He was safe in the hole he dug under the trailer, at least safe enough because the adults didn't know about it. Even if they did they couldn't reach him under the doublewide. He had an old school book bag hidden away as well, which contained what he considered his personal treasures—an old wallet with no money but it belonged to his mom in their happier days, a few pieces of Christmas candy he got a school party last year, a pencil, and an old rabbit's foot he had cut off of the dead animal in the road near his trailer. He hoped it would bring him luck someday. Russell settled down in his makeshift chair and pulled out the latest addition to his collection. A paperback book on crimes committed by soldiers. He had stolen it from the school library.

In his class at school, they recently finished up a unit on the Revolutionary War. Russell was fascinated with the soldiers and the weapons they used. His favorite was the bayonet. He could only imagine what it would feel like to drive the pointed end of the rifle into another person and watch the face of the victim as he realized he was going to die. Russell always pictured his mom's latest boyfriend in that role. Today Russell took great pleasure just thinking about the look that would be on old Fatso's face as he watched Russell drive the bayonet into his chest and twist and turn it until Wayne collapsed in a heap. Grinning and unconsciously rubbing the ear Wayne had bloodied, Russell felt a little better knowing he would be the ultimate master over Wayne. All he had to do was find a bayonet. Shaking his head out of his daydreaming, Russell opened his book to read. Ironically he discovered a passage about someone called "Mad Anthony" Wayne.

Mad Anthony was a survivor of the Paoli Massacre in 1777. The event occurred on a cool fall evening in Pennsylvania. American troops were asleep and a Loyalist sympathizer led some British soldiers to the encampment. Sneaking in and only using their bayonets, the Redcoats killed close to 200 American patriots. General Wayne was appalled at the attack and vowed revenge. Less than two years later he led an assault against a British fortification. The brutal attack lasted just 30 minutes and the soldiers were only allowed to use bayonets. When it was over close to 100 British soldiers were dead and another 450 plus were captured and doomed to spend their days in a prisoner of war camp.

Russell imagined being Mad Anthony and taking revenge on all the people who had harmed him. He turned to the last page of the book, grabbed the pencil and started making a list of anyone he thought deserved the fate of the bayonet. Topping the list was Wayne followed by the landlord. He thought about Ms. Edwards from his school. She used to make periodic visits to Russell's place which only made Wayne mad when she showed up. After the visit, Wayne would molest Russell. Russell associated Ms. Edwards with the sexual abuse so he included her on his list. Russell put the book in the backpack and hid it as best he could in the hole. It was starting to get dark outside and he didn't want to be under the trailer at night.

The next morning Russell got himself ready for school. He ate a dry bowl of cereal since there was no milk. He was used to the taste of the grain without milk and almost preferred it that way, plus he could grab some and go and not wait around the house for his mom or Wayne to get up. Fortunately, lunch was taken care of since his mom filled out the paperwork for him to get free lunches at school. At least he wouldn't go hungry. Russell hated being singled out though and made to feel like he owed everybody a big thank you just to get to eat lunch. He knew his mom could afford to make him lunch but she always spent her spare cash on drugs and alcohol. Russell vowed he would never get addicted to anything like that. He knew of a few kids in his grade at school who were already sampling their parents' stashes of booze. They all talked about it outside at lunch but they never included Russell in their conversations. To them he was non-existent which was fine by him because it made it easier to simply get through the long days at school.

The lunch hour wore on and finally the bell sounded for their afternoon classes. Russell liked the subject he went to next. Mostly he liked the teacher, Miss Teach. She was pretty and seemed to care about all of her students even Russell. Maybe especially Russell. She often stood by his desk when she was lecturing about history and smiled at him like they shared a secret or something. She had a way of making the stories come to life and Russell liked listening to her talk. She had a pretty voice, almost like she should be singing instead of talking. Russell wondered what it would be like if his mom were a teacher or if Miss Teach were his mom. He bet Miss Teach would never let her son eat dry cereal or have to eat a free lunch because she wasted her money on drugs.

Russell made his way to his desk and along with the other students settled down and got busy with their current assignments. Russell was writing in a journal as if he were a soldier from The Revolutionary War. The class had to create a magazine about the war and include diaries from people living at that time. The writings had to be fact-based but the students were allowed to make up people and their life stories to report the events. Russell had chosen to create a young soldier who left home to fight. He wrote about the soldier having a bad home life and escaping it to join the Continental Army. Writing about the bad home life was easy. He just used his own situation and wrote about his miserable existence.

Before long it was time to head home for the day. Russell quickly packed up his backpack and walked to the teacher's desk to leave his writing for her to grade. On her desk was a picture that Russell had seen many times. It was one of her and some man. She was smiling at the camera and the wind had blown her hair so that her bangs were across her face. Russell thought she looked just like a model, better even. Sneaking a quick glance at Miss Teach who was at the door saying goodbye to her students, Russell grabbed the picture and stuck it into his backpack and hurried out of the room.

Chapter 6
Libby

Elizabeth Teach, known to her friends as Libby, waved to the last student and then headed to her desk to settle down and read the journal entries of her previous class. She was particularly interested to read the one by Russell Thomas because she was worried about him. In previous assignments he always chose to write about violence and the darker side of human relationships. She had even voiced a concern about him to the guidance counselor, who didn't seem to care. Libby took the pile of papers and noticed Russell's was right on top. She picked it up and began reading about a soldier who was abused at home and escaped to the army and became a hero because of all the Redcoats he stabbed to death.

"Wow," Libby said out loud. "There has got to be something in that boy's life that makes him write like this." Not that anyone heard Libby but stating her concerns aloud seemed to put validity to her fears. She put his paper aside and read the others. She was looking to see if any of the other kids especially the boys, wrote so tragically. If any did maybe Libby would worry a little less about Russell, but if they didn't then she had serious issues with what Russell might be dealing with at home.

After about thirty minutes of reading the journal entries Libby made the decision to go and once again, voice her concerns to the school guidance counselor. This time she wasn't letting the matter rest until she got some kind of action from the advisor.

With the last name Teach it was destined that Libby would enter the profession. Fortunately, it fit in perfectly with her long rage of goal of becoming a criminal psychologist. She would teach while she was working on her graduate degrees. Libby loved inspiring young minds to grow and investigate the world in which they lived. She also loved history and made it enjoyable to her students by bringing the people alive with stories about their exploits. Her students loved it when she told them true stories about people like Andrew Jackson's mother and the time she marched into a British camp and demanded the return of her young sons. All of the kids could relate to an angry mom looking out for her children. This love of history resulted in noticing the unusual writing style and even the odd behavior of her young student.

During their recent study of the Revolutionary War, Libby noticed Russell was a bit too fascinated with the gory aspects of the war. Russell Thomas was in her sixth grade history class. He was normally a quiet child but the recent study on the weapons of the war brought out a side of him that had Miss Teach worried. He asked a lot of questions about the use of each weapon and especially the bayonet. He wanted to know how long it took the people to die and if they suffered. He even drew pictures on his papers of wounded or dead victims which had resulted from knife attacks. Normally an interest in weapons at this age wouldn't be of much concern since many sixth grade boys are just beginning to learn to hunt or fish. A fascination with the tools used for these activities was to be expected. But the morbid curiosity along with recent unexplained bruises on Russell and multiple absences from school, only served to cause Libby to worry that something was off in the young boy's life. It was her concern and observation of

Russell in class that had carried her multiple times to the guidance office. She was headed there again.

"Now Miss Teach, he is a 12-year-old, active boy. Bruises are to be expected." Ms. Margaret Edwards was the school counselor. Even though she had a masters in psychology and should understand unusual behavior, she was close to retirement and didn't seem to care about the children anymore, especially if it meant extra paperwork for her.

"But it's more than just bruises. I've noticed he seems to have trouble hearing and he never makes eye contact plus he has even limped a time or two," Libby said.

"Have you talked with his mom?" Ms. Edwards asked.

"Yes. I have called her plenty of times because his grades are suffering and he seems to have lost interest in school. Only recently has he even shown a hint of wanting to learn and that was on the weapons of the Revolutionary War which is another matter altogether." Libby had approached the counselor on numerous occasions expressing a concern that perhaps Russell was the victim of abuse at home. Ms. Edwards always explained it away. Libby's thought was that the woman just didn't want to get involved.

But Libby couldn't simply stand by and do nothing. The most recent sign of abuse was a bloody ear. In class Russell kept holding his head and when Libby told him to get busy with his work he moved his hand and she saw a tissue covered in blood. She promptly sent him to the school nurse. She gave him some pain killer and said there was nothing else to do. Once again his mom was alerted but she didn't seem concerned. She even sounded drunk when Libby called her.

"What do you want me to do?" said an exasperated Ms. Edwards.

"I want the authorities notified. How many seminars have we had to sit in about reporting signs of abuse and trauma? So I am following protocol and alerting you. Now, please report it to the police or child services.... somebody!"

"Miss Teach. It is not that easy to call in authorities and have a child removed. Often it can put a child in an even worse situation. Kids love their mothers and it is best to stay with them when possible."

Libby threw her hands up in dismay and in frustration yelled: "Seriously, you don't want to make a simple phone call?"

"Miss Teach, I'll have you know I have made multiple calls and visits in the past to this boy's home. You are not the first teacher to show concern over him. I have found nothing to cause undo worry or concern. His mom does her best and they both love each other. End of story." Ms. Edwards was equally frustrated with Libby and couldn't help but raise her voice to match Libby's.

"Well, this child's well-being is on you! I think things are much worse than you believe or were led to believe. When he ends up in the hospital or, heaven forbid, dead, I hope you finally feel some kind of compassion for him." Storming out of the room and fuming all the way to her car, Libby couldn't believe a school counselor would have such a lack of care for the students.

What neither of them realized was that every time someone showed any concern the consequences were very bad for Russell. The boy didn't want anyone coming to his house and talking to his mom and he especially didn't want anyone talking to Wayne.

One time last spring Ms. Edwards had paid a visit to Russell's home. She was there as a follow-up to some previous visits and to check on the cleanliness and food situation for Russell. After she left, Wayne took Russell out to the nearby woods and beat him badly, managing to avoid any facial bruises. Then he raped the boy and made him perform oral sex on him. Russell had never hated anyone as much as he did Wayne except for Ms. Edwards because in his mind it was her fault Wayne abused him. After he was finished, Wayne went back to the trailer to find Loretta already high and passed out. Wayne then drunk himself to sleep while Russell escaped into the woods. He stumbled upon a nearby neighborhood that was much nicer than his. While he was staring at all of the houses and imagining what it must be like to live in one, he saw a familiar vehicle turn down the street and pull into the driveway of one of the tidy homes. The car belonged to Ms. Edwards. Russell watched her get out of the car and carry a big purse and some groceries into one of the nearby houses. She put the bags down and looked under a flower pot for something. Evidently she kept a key hidden there. She unlocked the door and replaced the key then stood and looked around. Russell ducked even lower in the trees for fear she knew he was there. Just then he heard her call: "Here kitty, kitty. Puff, come to Mama" and a big tabby cat ran out from the front bushes and rubbed against her legs. Ms. Edwards gave the cat a pat on the head and let it in the house. Russell couldn't believe anything would willingly want to be around that old hag.

However, from that day on Russell felt some overwhelming compulsion to keep going over to her house and watching her. He got closer and closer to her house in his spying and even Puff the cat would come and rub against Russell while he was hiding in the bushes. Russell wasn't fond of cats and roughly pushed the animal away. The cat just kept coming back until Russell got so frustrated with it he picked it up and threw it into the street. The cat managed to get up before any cars came and limp away. He figured he'd have to teach the cat a lesson another way. It would serve Ms. Edwards right since it was her fault Russell got picked on so much.

Not long after the cat incident Russell was again hiding in the bushes. This time Puff came up and hissed and growled at him. Russell didn't want Ms. Edwards to come out and see what was going on so he simply choked the cat to death and buried her behind the bushes. Afterward Russell was feeling exceptionally bold so he got the hidden key from underneath the planter and snuck into in her house. Ms. Edwards was dozing on her couch and never knew he was there. Russell was able to sneak in many times after that and Ms. Edwards never suspected or caught on to his sneaky ways. No one in the neighborhood ever saw him.

Eventually Ms. Edwards quit coming out to Russell's house. Russell, on the other hand, didn't quit spying on Ms. Edwards. He had the feeling they would cross paths again in the near future. He just hoped Ms. Edwards didn't get any more cats. He didn't plan on killing any more pets but he would if he had to.

Libby took a deep breath as she exited the school. *How can I ever get through to him?* Her thoughts were on one student—Russell. She got in her car and drove to the café where she was to meet her boyfriend. She arrived before he did so she went in to get a table and wait on him.

Chapter 7
Mike

Mike O'Malley entered the café with one thing on his mind—Libby. He was looking forward to their dinner date and was completely oblivious to the gazes and turned heads directed at him. At 6'3" he was a handsome, blue-eyed blond, all-American looking guy. He was also incredibly fit and the police uniform he wore only enhanced his muscles. Mike and Libby had been dating since their freshmen year of college. Now as recent graduates they were both interested in establishing their careers before they tied the knot.

The female eyes in the room followed his progress across the café. Oblivious, Mike made his way to the booth where they usually sat. He smiled the moment he saw her. All eyes were on him as he joined a lovely woman with long, honey colored hair which framed her large brown eyes and dimpled face. They made quite a pair.

"Hey gorgeous. How was your day?" Mike greeted Libby with a chaste kiss on her cheek.

"Remember the student I told you about, Russell?" Libby said as Mike kissed her and she reached up to pat him on the cheek.

"Yes."

"Well, today he came to school with a big red knot on the side of his head. His ear was bleeding. I sent him to the nurse and after school I called his mom but she was obviously high or something. She didn't seem the least concerned. I also reported it to the school counselor, for all the good that did!" Libby sighed and took a drink of her water.

Silent Rage

The waitress appeared, ready to take their order. They both requested club sandwiches with sides of fruit and sweet teas.

Libby continued voicing her frustrations with the school system: "You know, we go to all these training seminars and have to take hours of classes that teach us how to recognize signs of abuse and what to do about it. So when I follow the guidelines I get nowhere. It's just so irritating! This boy shows classic signs of neglect and abuse and if someone doesn't intervene I shudder to think of what the future holds for him."

"What can I do to help you, Baby?" Mike held Libby's hands and caressed them as he listened to her talk about her day and concerns over her class. He loved everything about her, especially the way she cared about her students. This was the start of her third year of teaching. Mike was doing well with the police department and had future plans of becoming a detective. Maybe now was the time to start thinking about getting married.

"Well, I know you're not a detective yet, but do you think you could get some early practice and look into the boy's home situation? I know his mom does drugs and is often drunk when I call her. Here it is September of the school year and I already have made multiple phone calls to Russell's mom. I think her main job is dancing at the strip club and…"

"Whoa there, Libby, take a breath. You know I can't just investigate someone. That would be a violation of so many things. But what I can do is keep my eyes and ears open for anything concerning this family. I can drive by their residence and take a look."

Libby sighed and then gave Mike a smile revealing her perfect white teeth. "Thank you. Who knows, maybe you'll see his mom in the middle of a drug deal or something and you can arrest her. Surely there is a family member who could take in Russell and give him a better shot in life."

"Let's talk about something happier," Mike suggested.

"Are we still going to go look at houses on your day off?" Libby smiled at Mike.

"That's the plan. The realtor has several lined up and we just need to decide on one we both like. Then I can fix it up and get it ready for when you are living there with me."

"That sounds perfect. I am looking forward to seeing the houses."

Their sandwiches arrived and the two dug in with gusto and then talked about other things going on in their respective lives.

"All units in the vicinity of Spalding Avenue we have a 10-31. Code 2." Mike's radio alerted him to a possible drug deal underway. He was to proceed with caution and without lights and siren so as not to alert the potential dealers of his presence. Letting the dispatcher know he was enroute and requesting back-up, he gave Libby a quick hug and kiss when they reached her car.

"Be safe! I love you."

"Back at cha." Mike reached his cruiser, got in, then drove away.

Libby found herself with a few spare hours and no papers to grade so she decided to ride by Russell's home and do a little detective work herself.

Chapter 8
Russell

Russell ate another bowl of dry cereal. His mom hadn't gone to the grocery store and Wayne never fixed any meals. That was probably a good thing because Wayne was a pretty nasty guy. Even Russell noticed how dirty Wayne always was and he stunk most of the time. What his mom saw in this loser was anybody's guess. Russell returned the cereal box to the cabinet and looked around the small kitchen. He didn't want to leave any evidence he was home because then Wayne might want him to do the nasty. That was what Russell called the many sexual acts Wayne forced him to do. One time he had heard his mom refer to a coworker "doing the nasty" and Russell could tell his mom meant it was a bad thing. So every time Wayne made Russell do something he didn't like, in his mind he called it "the nasty."

Satisfied he had left no signs behind, Russell quietly opened the door and went outside to escape any potential meeting with Wayne. He had grabbed his school bag on the way out because he wanted to look at his latest treasure. Crawling under the trailer and settling down into his hiding place, Russell removed the photo of Miss Teach. *She sure is pretty,* he thought. He just stared at the picture and daydreamed about what life would be like with her as his mom.

When Russell heard a bunch of shuffling feet and voices coming his way, he quietly put his belongings back in the backpack and sat as still as he could. He sort of liked it when people hung out near his trailer while he was hiding underneath. He used these times to practice his soldier training. He pretended he was on a secret mission and if he was caught he'd be killed so silence was of the utmost importance. He got real still and just listened.

"I've got some good stuff coming and you're gonna be my first customers to sample it," said a guy wearing some dirty work boots.

"What kind of stuff?"

"Potent. You can get as high as you want. I've heard some can get so high they feel like they're in heaven and when they come down it's even a rush to settle back on earth." This was all a bunch of BS from the drug dealer. He didn't really know anything about this new substance and didn't care. He just wanted to make a sale.

Russell couldn't tell who was talking because all he could see were shoes. Most of them were dirty and torn and looked pretty cheap. Not the kind any good soldier would be caught dead in. One of the guys had on a decent pair of work boots even if they were a little dirty, and Russell figured he must be the leader of this crew. Russell knew these guys were not worth his time. A well-trained soldier knew when to let the enemy walk away. These guys were definitely not worth revealing his hiding place to, especially the guy wearing the decent work boots.

The dirty shoes were walking away and Russell could still hear their conversation.

"Get me some of this stuff and I want it tomorrow."

"I work tonight so I'll see what I can get as far as a sample. Bring me some cash and I'll let you get a little taste of glory."

The shoes were getting further away and Russell could no longer hear them very clearly. He knew they were talking about drugs. What he didn't know was it was a pretty lethal mix that would leave some of the boot-wearing guys dead.

Chapter 9
Libby

When Libby was a child her inquisitive nature frustrated her parents, yet they were proud of her spirit of adventure. Many times her parents were the ones cleaning up the messes Libby often found herself in or writing a check to pay for the chaos she caused.

One time when she was about eight years old Libby saw a bright red button that said "don't touch." So naturally she pushed it. The button was attached to a paint mixer and bright yellow paint spewed from the top of the machine.

'Oh no!' Libby gasped as she watch the yellow liquid spill like rays of sunshine all over the machine and the countertop and finally onto the floor where she stood. The young girl looked around for someone to help. Seeing a person who looked as if he worked here, she rushed over to the friendly looking man and admitted her mistake.

"So you accidentally pressed the button?" the man asked.

"No sir. I did it on purpose. I wanted to see what happened."

"Well, you made a mess is what happened."

"I know. I'm sorry and I'll clean it up if you just get me a mop and bucket."

"I think this is a bigger job than a little girl can handle."

"Oh, I'm not so little. I can clean that up easily."

The man chuckled. "I bet you could. But, no worries. I am going to get our janitorial staff to come and clean this right up. They have all the stuff required to do that and I can't allow a customer to risk slipping in it."

"Oh. I didn't think about all the trouble it would cause," Libby said as she looked down at her shoes.

"I'm sure you didn't and I bet you learned a lesson, didn't you?"

"Yes sir! I won't push any buttons that say don't push anymore." Libby smiled at the man as he walked over to a phone to ring for the cleaners.

Libby's parents heard the commotion and went to see what happened. They discovered Libby talking to the man they later found out was the manager. The stood nearby silently listening to their daughter admit her error. While they were irritated with Libby for causing the big mess, they were also proud of her for immediately finding the store manager, admitting her mistake, and volunteering to clean up the mess. Libby always had a strong sense of right and wrong and carried this trait into adulthood. Currently, Libby wanted to make things right for her worrisome student, Russell. She decided she needed to make a visit to his house.

Libby turned her bright red VW Jetta on the dark street where Russell lived. The only streetlight appeared to be burned out. The local residents had thrown so many rocks at the light breaking it that the power company no longer bothered to repair it. The residents of Spalding Avenue wanted their nocturnal activities to kept secret and were happy without the extra lighting. Libby was a bit naïve about human beings and always thought the best of people. She had no concerns for her safety even though the fact her shiny car, as well as being the lone occupant in it, sent an alert to the lookouts on the street. She didn't see the two darkly dressed males hiding in the shadows watching her progress. The only reason a single female would be on this street was because her john had lined up an appointment for her. Libby didn't even consider that she might actually be in danger when she called on any of her students at their homes, so she drove down the street oblivious to the menace hiding in the dark.

Driving slowly because she was looking for house numbers on the trailers, Libby finally found a place she thought was Russell and his mom's residence. She parked her car on the street, got out, and proceeded to the front door of the rusted brown and white glorified camper. The windows had striped awnings over them that would've been nice when they were new, but they looked like that was about fifty years ago. Now they were faded and torn and some hung in strips on the metal frames, like saliva on a rabid dog. Libby approached the cinder block steps and reached up to the door and gave it a quick knock. Before the door opened a tall and emaciated looking young guy appeared from around the back of the trailer.

"Wha' you want?" the living skeleton spoke loudly, startling Libby who turned to see who was talking to her.

"I am looking for Russell Thomas' home. I'm his teacher and I want to speak with his mom." Libby boldly stated her business to this fellow, whoever he was. "Are you a member of the family?"

For some reason that was funny to the guy and he replied, "She ain't got no kin other than that kid of hers. But I know everybody and everything that happens on this street so maybe I can help you." The skeleton walked closer to Libby and, in fact, got so near her she could smell his fetid breath. She involuntarily took a step backward but skeleton just stepped forward closing any gap between them.

"I just want to discuss a few things with his mom and really I don't need anyone else, thank you though." Libby said.

"Well, you can..." At that moment the door opened and pretty girl about Libby's age came out.

"Hey, shithead. Get out of here and leave the lady alone. Come on in, ma'am." Libby gladly escaped into the confines of the small house.

The girl slammed the door shut and turned to Libby. "I don't who you is or what you want. I only can't stand that prick harassing you. So you can wait about five minutes then get in your fancy car and get the hell out of my house."

Libby stammered in reply, "Oh well, uh, first of all, thank you for rescuing me and secondly, my name is Libby Teach and I am Russell's sixth grade teacher. Are you his sister?"

The pretty girl laughed, making a pleasant sound and said, "No. I'm his mother."

Libby tried to hide her surprise but must not have done a convincing job because Loretta angrily replied, "Don't look so shocked or like you ain't never had sex. I just got knocked up at 14 and didn't want to give the kid up. My own mom was a loser but I wasn't gonna' be like her. I thought a baby was the answer. But that ain't none of your damn business. Wha' do ya' want?"

"I wanted to discuss a few concerns I have about Russell and his school work as well as maybe anything that may be going on at home that I can help with."

"Everything is fine at home and in case ya' ain't noticed I am dressed and heading to work so ya' need to just go on and git. 'Sides, that counselor woman has called enough."

Libby had noticed Loretta's emerald green and very shiny halter top that tied around her neck and cupped her generous breasts. Nothing was left to the imagination as the material clung to every ounce of her size D's. The top stopped just above her bellybutton which was the home to a series of three delicate chains that dangled and had three arrows pointing to what might lie below. Her jean shorts were cut-offs that made Daisy Dukes' denims look like something a granny would wear. Clearly no undergarments were needed and Libby thought to herself this woman must spend a lot of time getting wax jobs. There was also a tattoo that was trying to sneak out of her shorts but Libby couldn't tell what it was other than to think it looked like the start of some sort of reptile. This girl certainly didn't look like any mother Libby had ever seen. None of her students had a mother who dressed like this and Libby's own mom was the complete opposite of the woman standing before her.

Libby's mom, Ann, had been a member of all the right clubs and social organizations. Libby was even presented as a debutante during the spring of her senior year in high school. Ann wanted to make sure all of her children had everything they needed in order to be successful in life. As Libby had grown and matured she came to genuinely appreciate the love and even sacrifice her mother gave to each of her three children. A college professor who still held classes, Ann was a role model whom Libby was proud to call mother. But at the moment, Libby was truly feeling sorry for this girl Russell had to call mom. Loretta must have picked up on the pity emanating from Libby and she began yelling at her to leave.

"I've asked you to leave. Now take your shitty judgmental attitude and get out of here." Loretta opened the door and pointed outside.

Libby opened her mouth to apologize just as the door to what must be the master bedroom opened and a man of about 30 wearing nothing but a pair of well-worn boxers appeared and demanded to know what the fussing was about. When the door first opened the smell of unwashed bodies and sex rushed out to assault Libby. The smell was so strong her eyes watered. "Loretta, you guys need to shut-up! I got to git up in the morning for my shift at the plant."

Loretta went over the man and gave him a big hug and kiss and said, "I'm sorry baby. Go on back to bed. I'm just leaving for my job and this here lady is Russell's teacher and she is leaving too."

"What's she want? Ain't nothing wrong with that boy. He's just dumb."

"Wayne, he is not and don't say that! You like him fine when he does things for you like scratch your back." At this comment red flags started rising in Libby's mind. She wondered just who this man was because as far as she knew there wasn't a father in Russell's life. So to have some unknown man apparently living here and calling the boy names just served to cause Libby to have more worries about the home situation for Russell.

Libby took a deep breath, so she didn't have to breathe too much as she approached Wayne, stuck out her hand to shake his and said, "Hello. I am Miss Teach and I am just making the rounds on my students at home so that they know I genuinely care about them and all aspects of their lives. Are you his dad?" She was well aware that this man was not Russell's dad she just couldn't think of any other way to get him to explain his presence in the home.

As Wayne took her hand he shouted, "Hell no, I ain't that turd's pa. But I'm the man of this here so called house and I'd like for you to leave now." With that statement he gave her hand a tight squeeze intending to cause her to sort of cower before him. Not one to back down, Libby returned his grip as hard as she could hoping to fend off any bruising. Mentally she cursed herself for ever wearing a ring on her right hand since now it was biting into her flesh. The pearl ring, which was a birthday gift from her parents one year, was cutting into her middle finger since the gemstone had a tendency to rotate when she wore it.

Loretta stepped forward and gave a tug on Libby's other arm and said, "We are leaving so go back to bed. Russell's out in the yard playing so just holler for him if you need anything."

The two women made their exit and Loretta turned to Libby and hissed, "I hope you didn't make things worse for us by showing up here. If it weren't for Wayne I wouldn't have any food for my table and that means neither would Russell. I owe him and I don't want no trouble. Just leave and you do your thing at school and I'll do my thing at home!"

Libby couldn't help but wonder what on earth a pretty girl like Loretta saw in the hairy, pot-bellied, unshaven, and no other word suited him but...jackass! She asked Loretta, "Who is that man though, and does he treat you and Russell ok? I am not sure that the two of you living here is a good choice. There are agencies that can help you. I'd be gl…."

"Bitch! What do you not understand? I said git and I mean it. Don't come back. I've got a good paying job and Wayne helps me with taking care of Russell. We got a roof over our heads and I don't want to mess it up. If he has to smack Russell to keep him in line, then that's ok. Kids today got too much freedom. It's like they're the damn adults anymore and my Russell respects us. Besides, it's all we got. Now you take your big shot ideas and your snobby ass and get out of my life and don't come back!" Loretta stormed over to her car, as much as she could in her four-inch heels, and drove off leaving Libby in a cloud of dust. She had no choice but to leave herself. As she started to open her car door the skeleton from before appeared beside her. It gave Libby a fright for him to just magically show up like that but she didn't want to act afraid.

"Lady, you ain't welcomed in my neighborhood so this one time I'll let you leave with no problems. You come back again and you won't be so lucky!"

Libby knew a threat when she heard one and for once she had enough good sense to simply get in her car and head home.

Chapter 10
Mike

While Libby was dealing with the walking skeleton, Mike was dealing with another kind of ghoul. Mike's was a living, well not anymore, replica of someone from a zombie movie. The kid was lying in a fetal position on the road at the back of a convenience store.

When Mike had first pulled up to the scene there was a crowd of onlookers but they all ran at the appearance of a police officer. A couple of other police cruisers arrived and the patrolmen took off after the fleeing addicts. Mike saw the body on the road and immediately radioed for EMS. The body was that of a Leo Kowalski aged nineteen and now deceased. Mike found out his name when he searched his pockets and found an old, faded wallet containing Leo's driver's license. Mike also found a baggie of a substance that appeared to be heroin. Mike assumed Leo's was a drug-related death and went through the proper procedures required in such a case. Leo must have convulsed and bit his tongue just about in half because there was congealing blood pooling from his mouth onto the road. It only served in making the body look like a dead vampire.

Mike secured the scene in case something was uncovered in the process of moving the body that would point to murder. From all Mike could see, everything appeared to be another random OD from an addict. Mike thought, *what a shame this guy's young life was now over. All for a brief high.* Drugs were bad in this area and it seemed like drug-related deaths were becoming a weekly occurrence. Mike knew he would probably be the one making the notification visit to a mother who was never going to see her son again. He hated that part of the job and no matter how many times he had to inform someone about a loss, it never got any easier. People reacted differently too. Some would scream and yell that it couldn't be their loved one and surely Mike was mistaken, while others politely thanked Mike for letting them know and quietly closed their doors to begin their mourning in private. Either way it was incredibly emotional to be with people when they received the news that would change their lives forever. He wondered what the next of kin would think about Leo. One time he had to make a notification and the victim's mother simply looked at Mike and said, "Well I can't say I'll miss the troublemaker. Can the state just bury him in some pauper's grave?"

Mike was speechless for a moment but told the woman he would pass along her request. He later heard that the victim had been cremated and his ashes placed in a box in a storage room where other unclaimed victims were placed until there were enough of them for a mass burial. Mike thought it was a sad way to end a life.

Mike watched as the body of the young addict was carted away in the back of the county morgue's van. It was time to go make the dreaded notification to whomever was at the address listed on Leo's driver's license. Mike had a feeling he would be talking to Leo's mother. Hopefully Mrs. Kowalski had some other family in the house with her.

"Hey, Jump! Let's go." Mike called for his partner to come and head out for the notification. Jump had been busy getting names and addresses of the survivors of the drug deal gone bad. He finally sent the last one off to lock-up and was ready to get away from the scene. After a long night of domestic disturbance and drug-related arrests plus the death notification, Mike finally made it home to his apartment for some much needed sleep. After just a few quick hours though, he was up for his next shift and doing the same thing all over again. Mike headed over to the station house for his shift. The midday briefing didn't really have anything new and unusual going on. Mike hope that the day would be a relatively calm one, that is, if such a thing even exists in the world of law enforcement.

Mike and his partner, Jump, whose real name was Frank Warren, suited up and headed out to their patrol car.

"Maybe we'll have a nice day keeping the fine folks of our community safe." Frank was nothing if not an optimist.

"We can hope. I'm guessing you want to head out for a quick bite before the day gets any longer." Mike knew his partner was always ready to eat.

"Got that right. Breakfast was hours ago and I feel like I'm wasting away." Frank grinned at Mike as the two pulled out of the station and headed to their go to place for food, Johnny's Burgers and Dogs.

The smell of hot burgers and French fries filled the patrol car with a much more enticing odor than what usually prevailed in the vehicle, which was usually the odors of unwashed bodies and vomit. The two police officers were immune to the smelly car and each took big bite of their respective meals and enjoyed a moment of culinary bliss. Just as they got their second bites into their mouth the dispatch radio shouted a call for officers to respond to a situation that involved drugs and gangs which was always a potentially dangerous and volatile mix.

With that Mike O'Malley and his partner, Frank Warren, buckled up and hit the siren. "Guess lunch is over," said Frank who was perpetually hungry and ate at every available break they had. He was a wiry 5'9 black man who grew up in a poverty-stricken neighborhood but wanted to give back to the area in a positive way. He joined the police force with the expectations of walking a beat and making his presence known. While he does get to periodically walk the streets, most of his time is spent riding in the patrol car and responding to calls. His eagerness to get out of the car and walk the beat earned him the nickname "Jump" because he usually jumped out of the car before it came to a complete stop.

"Jump, you'll survive a few hours without food."

"But I need my energy level up to deal with drugs and gangs, know what I'm saying'?"

Mike agreed he didn't like dealing with gangs in particular and there were always drug-related incidents surrounding gang activity. Spalding Avenue was the heart of one particular gang's turf where drug deals were made regularly. Mike and Jump had made numerous visits to the street. They had also made several arrests but the gang members seemed to multiply like flies on dead meat. They no sooner locked away one dealer when it seemed two others took his place.

"We can always hope we get lucky and get the real head of the enterprise. Maybe tonight we'll find out who he is." Mike said.

"Mike, my man, you are an optimist! These dudes ain't never gonna give up this guy. He pays 'em too much money plus he lets 'em run their prostitution ring as long as he gets a cut and a turn with the girls first."

"I can hope though. I hate seeing the kids on the street. It's like they're looking at their future. They always look depressed to me. I guess they have no hope for a better life." Mike had a soft spot for children. It always bothered him to see so many of them on the streets where the drug deals went down and the hookers left for their jobs in all manner of dress. No wonder the kids looked disheartened.

Jump agreed. Having grown up in a similar neighborhood he understood the mindset of the residents when it came to simply tolerating the gangs, drugs, and prostitutes.

The patrol car turned onto the street where the disturbance was located. The headlights of the unit highlighted the surprised faces of the gang members and the officers had a brief moment to try and identify any of them before they scattered like the maggots they were. Jump was already out of the car and chasing a gangly looking guy when Mike stopped the patrol car, got out, and pursued another man.

Mike's suspect was fast and knew the turf as well as the best paths to take in order to make a quick escape. He ran around one mobile home and Mike followed only to stop and look around trying to determine where the guy ran to. It was as if he simply disappeared into thin air. Not so much as a blade of grass was moving which would've pointed Mike in a direction to search. "Shit!" Mike was frustrated this lowlife could get away from him. It made him mad when he was outmaneuvered by some street punk. Mike took great pride in keeping himself fit and ready for anything that might come up when he was on patrol. Now he was just mad at himself for losing the guy.

As he turned to head back to the car and see where Jump was he heard a rustling sound from somewhere behind him. Turning to investigate the noise Mike realized it was coming from underneath the mobile home closest to where he was standing. He took his flashlight from his utility belt and shone it under the trailer. A young boy of about 10 or 12 was squinting into the glare of the light.

"Son, what are you doing under there? Come on out and head home. There's some trouble in the area and it's not safe for you right now."

The boy reluctantly crawled out and Mike got a good look at him. At first glance he saw a nice looking kid who sported the traditional buzz cut favored by preadolescent boys everywhere. However, upon closer examination of the youth, Mike noticed how dirty he was. His clothes were torn and looked a size or two too small. He was barefoot and his feet were filthy. There was what appeared to be the beginnings of a major bruise coming on his cheek just under his eye and he had dried blood stuck to his neck and on his shirt.

Mike asked him: "Kid, you ok?" The boy didn't answer and started to run away but Mike was quicker and caught him before he could get too far. "Why are you running? I just want to know if you're hurt."

Constantly squirming to get free the boy said, "I can't talk to you. If I do they beat up my momma and make her do bad things."

"Tell me your name and your momma's and I'll do my best to help."

"No, you can't, no one can. My momma's friend talked to the police and now we don't never see her no more. My momma thinks she's dead."

"I can keep a secret plus I can help. Now tell me who you are and who's your mom?"

"NO!" The boy gave his arm a good yank and broke free and ran deep into the dark trees surrounding the trailer park. Mike didn't chase him this time since he knew he wouldn't get any useful information from him.

Making his way back to the patrol car he found Jump leaning against it and with his hand resting on his gun. "Where you been pokey? I've already apprehended the asshole and he says he can help us. We'll see about that. With the amount of shit he had on his person he's looking at a long stretch. Seems he had some snow, hash, and even some brown sugar! Bet he wasn't gonna consume it himself either. He's looking at felony trafficking charges." Jump loved to use drug slang whenever he got the chance. He liked keeping up with the lingo so he could still talk with the guys from his old neighborhood. What Jump had discovered was said asshole had cocaine, marijuana, and heroin, which was some major stuff and brought in some major money.

Mike looked around the area and noticed it was strangely quiet and curtains were covering all of the windows in the surrounding mobile homes. "Looks like everyone has decided to mind their own business. Guess that's all we can do here. Let's take this scumbag in and you can tell me about it on the drive over." Mike nodded his head toward Bud. Jump grabbed the drug dealer and led him to the car.

"Move it, Bud. Get your ass in the car." Jump said.

Chapter 11
Bud

William Robert Budd, simply called Bud by everyone, was one of those unfortunate souls who just didn't get any help in the looks department. He had dark, deep-set eyes that were too close together, a large nose that resembled the shape of an overripe cucumber, and a bad case of adult acne. Only in his mid-twenties he had already lost whatever muscle tone he might have developed in his teens. All things considered he looked like a great big zit and he was ready to pop in order to save himself from a prison sentence.

Mike and Jump stood outside of the interrogation room and watched a couple of narcotics detectives attempt to talk to Bud.

"Come on Bud, just give it up and tell us where you got the drugs. We know you aren't smart enough to be the mastermind obtaining the supply but you are dumb enough to move it for him. So tell us where you got 'em and we can go easy on your charges." Raymond Smith was a hardworking, honest, and dependable cop. He had been around a while as a narcotics detective and usually had luck with his interrogations because he resembled everyone's favorite grandpa. But Raymond wasn't getting anywhere with Bud.

"I'm not telling you anything. I want to talk to the guys who brought me in. I'll only talk to them or I'm requesting my lawyer!"

Raymond's partner, Al Wilson, shoved his chair back as he abruptly got up. "Fine! Have it your way but those guys can't help you like we can." Al left the room and stopped off at the soda machine to get a can of his favorite drink, Mountain Dew. Al was also a seasoned detective who was good at his job and his only vice was his love of the soda which gave him a nice pot-belly and made him the object of many wise cracks from his fellow officers. He popped his drink and took a big swallow as he walked up to Mike and Jump.

"You guys see it all?"

"We did. Jump is the one who caught him and says he planned to talk. Wants to be an official snitch 'cause he claims he can't survive in prison." This from Mike who put some coins in the machine and then gulped down an entire bottle of water in one thirsty swallow.

"He's got that right. He's so butt ugly somebody would for sure make him a bitch just so they can look at his ass instead of his face." Jump was not one to sugarcoat anything.

Al finished up his soda and gave a big belch filling the hall with the smell of Mountain Dew. "OK, you guys have at him. See what you can get. You wanna make him a confidential informant? We could use one from the Spalding area. That place is a cesspool."

Mike also finished his water and tossed the bottle into the recycle bin but he skipped the burp. "Sure. We'll talk to him and see what we get. We have to go out to that area at least three to four times a week. I know there are kids around. Maybe this loser can do something good for a change and help his neighborhood clean-up their act. Having a CI can only help."

Raymond walked and up and heard the end of the comment: "Good luck with that! That neighborhood has been trouble for as long as I can remember."

Mike and Jump entered the interrogation room. Bud sat up straighter and smiled revealing his few remaining teeth. "So you guys wanna deal?"

"No, we don't want anything to do with you. But I care about the city and want to get losers like you off the street. If I have to let you be a CI so I can help some kids have a future, then I'm willing to try. But one slip up and I'll haul your ugly ass to prison and tattoo 'bitch for sale' on your face and leave you in gen pop." There were times Mike really appreciated the way Jump could cut right to the chase. The two men spent the next hour setting up Bud as their new informant for the Spalding Avenue area. They gave him one month to produce something useful or they'd pick him up for a one-way trip to prison.

Bud called a friend to come bail him out. The police did all they could to make it look like Bud was getting released on a technicality. This protected Bud in his neighborhood and even gave him more street credibility. His drug sales would spike. Go figure why people trust a guy with a record to give them something they plan to put in their body in some manner.

Chapter 12
Russell

Russell ran away from the cop and locked himself in the bathroom of his mobile home. He cleaned himself up and got ready for bed. He wanted to hide under the covers and stay away from Wayne. Russell had gotten pretty good at being quiet and stealthy. Partly from a desire to be invisible to Wayne and partly from a desire to practice being a soldier, Russell was able to sneak into bed and finally fall asleep. He had dreams of what life would be like if he lived in a nice house and had someone like Miss Teach for his mother. Russell bet she would never forget her kid's birthday. Tomorrow Russell turned 13. No one would celebrate it and no one would throw him a surprise party. In fact, no one even knew it was his birthday. Russell choked back tears and fell into a dreamless sleep.

The next morning when Russell got up for school, he quietly got another bowl of dried cereal, still no milk in the house, and saw the door to his mom's room was closed. He knew Wayne left for his shift at the plant at 6:30. Looking out of the dirty kitchen window Russell could see his mom's car parked by the trailer. He knew she'd be asleep for hours. She probably wouldn't even get up until it was time to get ready for her job.

Russell gathered his backpack and went out the door closing it quietly behind him. His mom may not even remember it was his birthday but he knew she needed her rest and he didn't want to wake her. He whispered "Bye, Mom" and headed off to the bus stop.

"Hey, look everybody! Here comes the retard," said a boy known as the neighborhood bully. He had a gang of guys that hung out with him. Not because they necessarily liked him but more because they would rather be friends with him than the recipient of his abuses.

Russell slowly made his way to the bus stop but tried to keep his distance from the bully. He still got shoved by some of the others while he waited. One of the other kids knocked the book bag Russell was carrying to the ground. Russell quickly bent to retrieve it before they could take it from him.

The bully tried to grab the backpack but Russell held on tightly and told the kid to leave him alone.

"Guys, retard wants me to leave him alone. Maybe I should just show him who's boss around here." The other kids were agreeing with the bully and urging him to hit Russell.

"Just leave me alone. I didn't do anything to you," Russell said as he tried to show he wasn't afraid.

"Aw, baby wants to be weft awone," said the bully.

"Back off." Russell was getting madder at the guys and his anger was making him more and more bold. "You'll regret it if you don't leave me alone."

"Why, I oughta," but the bully didn't get to finish his remark. The bus pulled up saving Russell from any more confrontation with the guy, at least for the time being.

The kids piled into the bus and Russell sat close to the driver because he knew the others would leave him alone when he sat in the front. The doors closed and the bus took off for school. Russell had a few minutes of peace before arriving at school and trying to avoid any more bullies.

Chapter 13
Lucky Sam

Lucky Sam earned his name the hard way. As a kid growing up in the projects he managed to get into his fair share of trouble. But it was like he had a guardian angel or something because he never got in serious messes even though most of his friends did. They all taunted him with name calling and told him he was just plain lucky he didn't get his own ass hauled to juvie like they did.

His mom looked the other way at all of little Sam's escapades. She just said, "Boys will be boys," which really just served to make her own conscious feel better because her oldest boy was already known as the go-to guy in the neighborhood when someone wanted drugs. He'd already been arrested a couple of times but they were minor issues so he was back on the street pushing dope without hardly missing a sale. Sam's mom barely made ends meet with her job as a school custodian. So when her oldest boy brought home extra cash and paid for school clothes and food for her and Sam, who was she to complain.

Sam looked up to his big brother, McKenna. Everyone called him Mac because McKenna didn't seem to fit the image of a drug dealer. When Sam followed Mac around on his runs he saw how the girls always smiled at Mac and flirted with him and promised him all sorts of fun later in the evening. Sam was just reaching puberty at this time and was envious of all the female attention Mac received. One night when Sam had just turned thirteen, Mac called over a particularly pretty girl and handed her a baggie with some weed and a twenty dollar bill in it. He told her his little brother was called lucky but he'd never been lucky if she knew what he meant. She said she did and took the packet in one hand and with the other she pulled Sam with her and introduced the boy to the pleasures of sex. Sam bragged the next day that now he really was lucky. All of his buddies were jealous. The lucky moniker stuck and he's been known as Lucky Sam for a couple of decades.

It didn't take too many more years for his big brother's luck to run out and he was caught with a kilo of coke on him and he was sent away for a long time. Mac's luck continued to spiral down in prison and finally ended when he was killed in the shower by some other inmates who used a homemade shiv on him.

At the funeral, Mac's mom was in tears not so much because her oldest boy was dead, but more so because her source of any extra income was gone. Lucky Sam, who was just getting ready to graduate high school, put his arm around his mom. "Don't worry, Mom. I am gonna take over Mac's business. I am going to take care of you even better than Mac did.

She reached up and patted Lucky on the face and simply said, "Bless you."

Lucky Sam kept his word and by the time he was twenty his mom was able to retire from the school and enjoy relaxing in her new apartment located away from the projects. She spent her days watching her favorite soap operas and going to her church for Bible studies. She always prayed her son's luck would hold out. Her prayers seemed to work. Lucky Sam's business grew. The demand for drugs was on the rise and Lucky took full advantage of it. He branched out into selling designer drugs, he had girls he pimped out, and he even loaned out money. Of course he did so at an extremely high interest rate. Usually the people who needed the money were also the ones who needed to support their drug habit so it was a win-win for Lucky Sam.

Sam finally moved his business into a building and hired even more girls. Located not far from the trailer park where Loretta lived, the area was home to multiple nightclubs and therefore, the lowlife often associated with those kinds of places. Sam's luck continued to follow him and his joint did a booming business over its rival neighbors. Probably because it was the lone so-called gentlemen's club in the city. Sassy A's was the place to go to see pretty girls strip dance as well as pay for a chance to conduct some behind the scenes one-on-one time with the girls.

Lucky Sam owned the joint and he originally called it Sassy Ass but the city wouldn't grant him a business license with that name. So Sam just shortened the Ass to A but everybody knew what the A meant. Nowadays he could probably get a license with the word ass in the title but why bother. Sassy A was successful and the patrons didn't care what it was called as long as they got what they wanted. And they did. Lucky Sam made sure his customers could get whatever their twisted hearts desired and he had the girls to do it. He had even expanded into including some guys for the guests with homosexual proclivities.

Lucky Sam even had one drag queen dancer and he was one of the most popular shows.

The dancer was known as Curly Shirley and he had a head of beautiful black tresses that were all his. No enhancements needed, at least not on his head. Shirley was also a favorite among the girls backstage because he looked out for everybody as if they were his own flesh and blood. He had been thrown out of his parents' house when he came out of the closet and told them not only was he gay but he also liked women's clothes and he wanted to dance in them. With nowhere to go and no one to claim as his own, his fellow strippers became his surrogate family. Curly Shirley was becoming very worried about Loretta. Lately she was high more than she wasn't and she would rather spend her time in a drug-induced fog in a back room with paying customers than dancing on stage. Loretta was a good dancer and made a lot of money but she was trading in the cash for the drugs.

Shirley tried to talk to her about her addictions but she just told him to back off and mind his own business. Loretta was currently in one of the back rooms with a customer. Shirley was confident this particular customer was the one bringing in crack to Loretta and if Lucky Sam found out someone was using outside blow in his own establishment it would not end pretty for the violator. Hopefully Sam would go easy on Loretta since he seemed to have a soft spot for her.

No sooner had Shirley thought about the consequences than his door burst open and Lucky Sam's two hired enforcers were standing in the opening. "Where's the dude at?" The one called Albert asked. The two men were brothers and their mother had given them the unfortunate names of Albert and Dalbert. Supposedly the names meant something about being bright and famous. That couldn't have been farther from the truth in Shirley's opinion and most everybody else's opinion too. The two Berts, as they were called, were simply big and dumb. The perfect combination to be the muscle behind Lucky Sam.

They did whatever he asked and that often meant beating someone up—their favorite thing to do—and was only surpassed by an order to get rid of a problem. Shirley always tried to play nice with this duo for two reasons. One, he was very afraid of them and two, he wanted them on his side if he ever needed their services.

"Hi fellas! The gentleman you're looking for is in one of the backrooms but I am not sure which one." He really did know but he was hoping to be able to somehow alert Loretta to the trouble headed her way. Shirley followed the two guys into the hall and proclaimed loudly so as to warn Loretta: "I think they're in the room at the very back or they could be in the champagne room."

"We done checked there," said one of the Berts.

Loretta was in the room next to Curly Shirley and well on her way to being a zombie but something in her mind clicked when she heard the deep voice of Bert.

"Hey, you gotta get out of here now." Her words were slurred and her companion was about as coherent as she was. Loretta tried to shove the guy off the bed and managed to get his feet to hit the floor.

"Wha's wrong? Ain't you having fun?" Loretta's evening delight was slowly coming to and both of them realized at about the same time he needed to get out of the room right then. The man looked around frantically for a place to hide or a window to go through and finally found one behind some heavy drapes. Just as he attempted to lift the window the two Berts slammed into the door and burst into the room. Loretta quickly ran out of the room and into the changing area and got ready to get on stage. She was hoping this would calm Lucky Sam down and he wouldn't be upset with her.

"I didn't do anything!" cried the man the two Berts were dragging out from the curtains and stood him in front of Lucky Sam.

"I know you brought some of your own blow which you did not purchase from me or one of my boys here," Lucky Sam said as he nodded at the two Berts.

"I didn't know you had any. It was just something to help set the mood for me and the girl."

"Seems you just admitted to having the stuff when you at first said you didn't do anything. So I can only assume you brought it in and didn't have no respect for my establishment. I don't like that. There's a fine you have to pay." Lucky Sam said to the scared addict.

"OK, OK. I'll pay whatever. Just let me go."

"Oh, I don't need your money. But my boys here need a good workout and you're gonna provide them the means to do so." Both Berts gave a soft laugh at Lucky Sam's comment.

"Boys, take this piece of garbage outside. You know I don't allow nothing rough to go on in the office." Lucky Sam slowly made his way toward the wanna be drug dealer. "I hear you're bringing your own candy into my joint. I don't like that. I think it's rude and I'm gonna let my two boys here teach you a lesson in club etiquette. Fellas, you take this here loser and let him know who owns this office and what is considered appropriate behavior. Let him live so he can spread the word but otherwise he's all yours."

The two Berts grinned and each grabbed an arm of the poor guy and carried him out a back door. He was screaming like a girl the whole way. All the dancers just turned and went back to work. Lucky Sam went into the dressing room and found Loretta. As he approached her he smiled and lifted a big finger to gently stoke her cheek. "Sugar, I know you was using some of that guys crack. And you know I can't allow that in my own office."

"I know and I'm sorry. It won't happen again."

"You're right it won't happen again, but you got yourself addicted to the junk. I can't have my best dancer not performing and I also can't let you not suffer some consequence. This is your only warning and I got to do something to send a message to the other girls. So because I like you and you're like my kid sister I'm gonna let you pick your punishment."

Loretta was already squirming under the mean gaze of Lucky Sam. He might say he loved her like a sister but Loretta knew her days were numbered if she didn't straighten up. When Lucky Sam gave you a choice you'd better choose well or he would just make you suffer all of the consequences. Her choices were a slash on the face, not an option for someone who makes her living off her looks, a busted kneecap, also not an option for a dancer, or a broken arm. It was her only choice. "I'll take the arm." Loretta told Lucky Sam with tears running down her face.

"I thought you might pick that one. As soon as the boys get back inside I'll tell 'em and then they'll get you looked at. You still gotta perform tonight so expect to stay late." With that said, Lucky Sam left the room and went to inform the Berts of their next order of business.

The first victim of the Berts was left in the alley behind Sassy A's. He was breathing but just barely when the boys finished with him. On their way inside they decided to move him to the establishment right beside Sassy A so they dragged him over to the back step of the

Chinese restaurant and left him there for the cooks to deal with. Next, they went to have a meeting with Loretta.

In the kitchen at Sassy A, Bud was busy trying to listen as well as keep working so he wouldn't make Lucky Sam mad. Clearly the big man was in a bad mood.

"Yo, Bud! Get over here." Lucky Sam bellowed from his office down the hall.

Bud dried off his hands and quickly appeared before his drug supplier.

"I am in no mood for any of your lip. This is how it's going to be. I have some product I need you to move. It's a trial batch and if you move it such that I make a sizable profit, I may let you in on a steeper cut. I don't care what your personal creed is about selling new drugs, I am simply telling you how it's going down. You got a problem?"

"No sir, Boss. I'll start pushing it right away to my regulars." Bud didn't know how he was going to keep Lucky Sam off his back, his regulars alive, and the police informed. He was sincerely wishing he had just gone to prison.

"Here ya' go. I'm calling it Lucky Sam's Green Speed. The first of what I expect to be a very lucrative venture for us…. or else." Lucky Sam chuckled at this last comment as he tossed a duct-taped package to him. Bud went cold inside.

Chapter 14
Loretta

Loretta tried to sneak into the trailer without anyone hearing her but her new cast wouldn't allow her to hold the door and ease it closed. Bam! Loretta cringed when she heard it slam. She knew it would wake up Wayne and now she would have to deal with him. Her arm was killing her. The doctor who treated her after the Berts broke her arm would only give her a mild painkiller.

"I'm only giving you a trivial dose of sedative since I know you have some other drugs in your system right now," said the doctor Lucky Sam kept on his payroll for these under the table type jobs.

"I only had one hit of cocaine and that was just so I could stand being with the loser who brought it."

"That's not what I'm told. Evidently you are using more and more of these illegal drugs. You must know it won't end nicely for you if you keep using."

"Don't try to preach at me. You've got no idea what my life has been like. I am doing all I can to keep food on the table for me and my boy. Now just finish up so I can get home and take care of my kid." Libby wasn't really worried about Russell. She was more interested in finding some of her private stash she had hidden in the trailer. It would take the pain away.

The doctor just looked at Loretta and shook his head. He knew Loretta would probably go find something else to take. He didn't want an OD on his conscience but he could only do so much for Loretta. He gave her directions on taking care of her arm and then sent her on her way. By the time she made it home she was tired and simply wanted to sleep.

"Loretta, that you?" Wayne was obviously awake now.

"Yeah, baby. I'll be right there."

"I'm ready for some of your special massaging so bring some of that Jack Daniels." What Wayne wanted was for Loretta to pour the whiskey all over his crotch and proceed to lap it off him like a dog.

"Damn." Loretta cursed as she grabbed the half empty bottle and carried it into the small bedroom.

"What happened to you?"

"Nothing. I tripped off the stage at work and broke my arm." Of course, Wayne wouldn't know that was a blatant lie.

"I always tell you what a klutz you are. Oh well, as long as you got another arm we's ok for some fun before I have to get my shut-eye to be ready for my shift. Now take off them clothes so I can look at them titties while you play Dr. Jack with me." Inwardly Loretta groaned and outwardly she took off her clothes for what felt like the millionth time that night.

In the room next to Loretta's, Russell heard the exchange between the two adults. It sickened him and he hated for his mother to have to do those things to Wayne. Russell plotted in his mind all the ways he could kill Wayne and get away with it.

"One of these days I should just gut him with my knife. Or maybe I could fake tripping into him and stabbing him in the crotch. Then I could just take the blade and run it right up his fat belly and his insides would fall out like a pig."

Silent Rage

It was those dark thoughts that helped Russell ignore the moaning coming through the thin walls and lull him into a fitful sleep.

Chapter 15
The Berts

While Russell was being serenaded with the nighttime sounds of coupling from Wayne and Loretta, Lucky Sam was busy conducting some of his own nocturnal activities.

"Hey, Berts! Get yo' asses in here." Lucky Sam bellowed for the two bouncers to come to his office.

"Yeah, Boss?" Albert, the more articulate of the two Berts, asked. Both Berts entered the room dressed in matching black shirts, jeans, and leather jackets. The tee shirts they wore had a pocket over the left breast. The Sassy A logo, a gold geometric figure in the shape of a pear and with a solid line right down the center, was imprinted there. It might be in the shape of a piece of fruit but everyone knew it really represented the A in Sassy A.

"You know that problem you took care of earlier?" Lucky Sam was referring to the poor sucker who was left for dead in the ally

"Yeah, we made sure the message was delivered with the proper force." Albert snickered and punched his twin in the stomach as he replied.

"Yeah, that guy. Seems he has access to a piece of land that houses some good product. I want you two to go confiscate it for me. Understand what I'm sayin'?" Lucky Sam rarely stated exactly what he wanted accomplished just in case someone ever decided to snitch on him. All anyone would have would be a bunch of vague conversations.

"Yeah Boss. We got this." The two Berts smiled and left the office to go do Lucky Sam's dirty work and were quite happy to get to do so. They headed out to the parking lot and got in their black Escalade. In the back, covered by a tarp, was an assortment of tools they would be using for their assigned task.

The Escalade purred along the road in relative silence. The Berts liked to keep their SUV in tip top shape. It was a nice car and was loaded with all the bells and whistles. These two were well compensated for their job. This particular excursion was taking them out into the boondocks well away from any homes or neighborhoods. They were heading to a place called Candie's Acres of Flowers. It was a spread of just over 600 acres. The business boasted that they supplied all the daisies needed for anyone within a 200-mile radius. They also had a nice website where they were expanding into shipping bulbs anywhere in the world. However, this was not their main money maker and neither was the 600 acres the extent of their establishment. The real size of their operation was closer to 1000 acres, it's just that Candie's Acres of Flowers didn't want Uncle Sam knowing about the other 400 acres. But it was this area that interested Lucky Sam.

Spread over the unreported 400 acres were some of the most beautiful and lush green plants a person would ever see. These plants were worth their weight in gold since they were marijuana weed. Candie and her family willing packaged the verdant plant and sold it to enterprising dealers who were willing to pay a premium to get the goods and to keep their name out of any records. Just like the floral aspect of the business was expanding, so was the drug division. Recently Candie and her clan had ventured into the cocaine market. A regular client of theirs, known only to Candie as Tommy, who also dealt cocaine on the side, went to Candie and said he'd be willing to give her a cut of the profits if she gave him access to her marijuana customer list. Candie is nothing if not a shrewd business woman. She agreed to the terms and set about discovering who the cocaine buyers were and before long she had a good idea of how to market the powder herself. She figured she could run it just as good as anybody. Ironically and at about the same time Candie decided to take over the cocaine aspect of the business, her marijuana-using cocaine-dealing customer quit showing up. Rumors say one of Candie's nephews helped the guy move to a new place, about six feet under over in the marijuana field. Candie was pleased with her lucrative venture and didn't care what her customers did with the product as long as they purchased it from her. It was one of these new customers that took the addictive substance into Lucky Sam's place and proceeded to give some to Loretta. That guy only got a severe beating and a few broken bones, but the Berts had much more in store for Candie and her family.

The Escalade made a quiet entrance onto the remote property. The Berts may be the meanest SOBs around but they definitely weren't the smartest. It didn't even cross their minds that a place trying to stay under the radar of law enforcement might have their own sort of radar to alert them to any unwanted and unwelcomed visitors. A very expensive security system was in place to let the owners know when someone was nearby. Neither Bert saw the cameras camouflaged in the trees. The machines were sending real time videos to a member of the family who was charged with being the lookout for the evening. Tonight the guard was one of Candie's sons.

Silent Rage

Candie's family was quite large, as in not only were they big in stature but also there were a lot of them and they were heavy in the testosterone department. Candie was the only daughter of a farmer who served his country proudly during the Korean War and even came back with a couple of mementoes. One of those was a medal Ray Flowers received due to his quick reaction at tossing back an unexploded hand grenade which spared the lives of about ten other guys in his unit. The grenade, in return, landed in the literal lap of the Korean who had originally tossed the malfunctioning device sending him and a few of his buddies onto Korean Heaven, wherever that was. The other memento Ray brought back was an addiction to marijuana. He loved getting high and feeling good. Ray thought if he liked it so much others would too so he set about turning his farm into the go to place for cannabis. He knew the government would not take too kindly to his selling the weed out in the open so he used an inspiration from his name to open up a business and started growing flowers. He settled down and married a nice local girl who gave him four strapping young boys and one sweet little daughter who was the apple of his eye. Ray had long since gone onto his own heaven and left the farm to Candie, who turned out to be the only one in the family with enough brains to run the operation. Now Candie was the boss and she had her own family of four sons. Her brothers had also carried on the family tradition of having sons and provided ten more boys between the original four brothers. Needless to say with all the testosterone and the marijuana, aggression and violence was simply how they got things done.

The Berts didn't know the Flowers' family history. Maybe if they did they would've handled things a bit differently, but then again, probably not. They weren't the brightest bulbs out there. As it was, the two thugs just proceeded straight out to bash some heads around, maybe cause some serious bodily harm, and, if they were really lucky, they might even get to use some of their new assault rifles. When they reached the nursery they drove right up to what looked like the main building of Candie's Acres of Flowers and stopped their vehicle. They didn't immediately get out and that's what probably saved them. Dalbert was driving when he heard a ping coming right off the front windshield. One of their bells and whistles for the SUV was bullet proof glass. In their line of work it was a necessity and right then it saved their ugly mugs.

"Damn, I think we done been shot at." Dalbert said to Albert.

Both Berts pulled their handguns out and ducked lower in the seats as they scanned the area for the shooter. Also stored underneath their seats was a secret compartment where some extra ammo for their handguns was stashed along with a couple of sawed off shotguns. They got these out as well.

"I can't tell where the guy is but I'm guessing somewhere near the house. We need to get out and find this mother and take care of him."

"How we gonna do that?" Dalbert asked as he inspected his weapon.

"We just gonna open the doors at the same time and see which one gets shot. The other one of us runs to them trees over there and takes a survey of things. Maybe shoot at him and then the other of us can run and join up at the trees." The two Berts agreed to the impromptu plan and counted to three and opened their doors. A shot rang out to the driver's side so Dalbert rolled out of the door and ran to the trees. He made it just as a shot rang past him. He returned fire and Albert was able to run over and hide as well.

Just as the two Berts caught their breath they noticed a few more bodies had shown up on the porch of the building.

"It looks like they got reinforce..." Dalbert didn't get to finish his thought because the so called reinforcements started plastering the SUV with assault rifles. The barrage went on for what seemed like an eternity but was probably just a few minutes. When it stopped and the smoke had cleared the guys could see that the car had been sprayed with bullets and had so many holes it resembled a giant chunk of black Swiss cheese.

The Berts were in a state of shock and were slowly realizing that their means of escape was gone. Not to mention their beloved car was totaled which just pissed them off even more. Not being trained in any kind of tactical assault, the two Berts just ran off of rage. They looked at each other and then roared as they came out of hiding with guns blazing. Calling them lucky was an understatement. They caught the Flowers boys off guard and were able to take down three of the four. The remaining guy dropped his gun and held up his hands. Stupid.

"You shouldn't a shot up my ride." Dalbert said to the trembling teenager.

"Get us a vehicle, now!" Albert used his rifle to point at the scared boy. Randy Flowers was all of nineteen.

He hadn't lived long enough to see the evil that comes with being in the drug business. He figured if he got the two large men a car then they'd leave and he'd be fine. Again, stupid.

Randy got the keys to a late model truck and started to toss them to one of the Berts.

"No first show me where it's at." Albert was still using the rifle to make his point.

The scared youth led the two Berts to the side of the building where a parking lot was located containing some work trucks.

"It's the big black one over there." Randy trembled as he pointed to where the pick-up was parked.

"Get in."

The three climbed into the truck and Randy started it up. He figured the guys wanted him to drive them safely off the property.

"Now get us over to the part where the weed grows."

The truck took off and drove about five minutes away. Once in the area the Berts had Randy get out of the truck. Off to the west of the truck was a dark and dilapidated shack. At first glance it looked like an old abandoned cabin. But when Albert walked over to the shed and noticed a shiny lock and chain on the door it made him figure there was something inside he wanted to know about.

"What's that building over there?" Dalbert asked the trembling Randy.

"It's nothing, just a place to store fertilizer." Randy thought he could still talk his way out of this mess.

"You're shittin' me. Ain't no way you have stuff for them flowers this far out. I'm thinkin' it may really be fertilizer but the kind my boss sells once it's tweaked a bit."

"I don't know what is in there for sure. I never go in. My uncles have the key and are the only ones allowed in. They told me it was fertilizer."

Albert decided to investigate but just as he proceeded to go up the steps of the front porch a large, black beast of a dog came flying around the side of the building. The muscular Doberman was running straight for Albert. As the dog got closer Albert did what comes naturally to him which was to simply point his gun and shoot the attacking animal. He caught the dog in the chest just as the animal was preparing to jump up and attack Albert. The animal died on the spot and fell in a bloody heap at Albert's feet.

Albert kicked the dog out of the way and then shot the lock off the door. He walked in and discovered a state of the art drug lab. He chuckled to himself and said, "Boss is sure gonna be happy with this place."

Albert walked out of the building and yelled over to Dalbert, "Yo, bro! We just found us a redneck chemistry set!" Just as soon as he said it a shot rang out and splintered the door frame right beside him.

"Damn!" Both Berts ducked and ran for cover. Dalbert pulled Randy behind the truck.

"Tell 'em to quit shootin' that you's just showing us around." Dalbert waved the gun at Randy who yelled out to the shooters to stop, it was just him.

"Randy? What are you doing over here? You know it's off limits." Uncle Hank stepped out of the shadows. "You target shooting out here? I heard shots."

"I was just curious and was showing my friend our product." For a scared boy Randy was doing a good job of improvising. It allowed the Berts to take aim at the voice and as soon as they caught sight of him a single shot rang out and pierced the middle of Uncle Hank's forehead. He fell to the ground and Randy gave a short yelp at losing another member of his family.

"How many more relatives you got?" asked Dalbert.

"The rest are sleeping. They take turns patrolling the place and tonight was Uncle Hank's shift. You didn't have to shoot the dog." Randy said as he wiped his nose.

"It was him or me so, yeah I did." Albert had already forgotten about the dog.

"Dalbert, I think we need to take care of this and head back to alert Boss. You ready?"

"Yeah, I am. Me first?" Dalbert and Albert had a sort of communication only twins can understand and they each seemed to know what the other was thinking. The two had agreed to go and inform Lucky Sam about things but only after they took care of Randy. Then while Albert held the gun on Randy, Dalbert proceeded to beat the young man to a pulp. When Dalbert paused to take a breath and look at his handiwork, he was pleased to see that, in his opinion, no one would know who Randy was. His face resembled a red chunk of beef. Poor Randy was indeed unrecognizable. His nose was broken as was his right cheekbone and jaw. His eyes were swollen shut and it looked like a few teeth were on the ground. He had at least two cracked ribs and he was coughing up blood from the damage inflicted to his lungs.

"Save somethin' for me, Dal."

"OK, I'm about done I think. Have at 'im."

Albert then simply walked around to the back of Randy, placed the gun to his head and pulled the trigger. Randy's head exploded.

"Shit, I got blood on me." Albert complained.

"What we gonna do with his body?"

Albert looked around and noticed the woods nearby. "Let's put him in there and let nature take care of him."

"What about the guy over there?" Dalbert nodded to the dead Uncle Hank.

"We'll just make a family plot." Both brothers laughed at that.

The Berts dragged first one body and then the other into the woods and attempted to hide the corpses under an old log and some bushes. The last thing they did was to pull the dead animal to the side of the building.

"Now, let's go deliver the boss's message to the family along with our condolences."

They drove off in their new truck and stopped by their demolished SUV to retrieve any weapons that were still salvageable. They then calmly called and informed the family they were no longer in the business of selling drugs. They didn't care about the flowers but the weed and the meth lab now belonged to Lucky Sam and he would be collecting his money soon. The family was also told that Lucky Sam knew what the going rates were for drugs and he expected payment in full. Any attempts at cheating the boss would result in a death a day until the family was no longer part of planet earth.

Chapter 16
Mike

Mike and Jump got a call to head out to an area with a known gang presence as well as a huge drug problem. This kind of call was always dangerous and both Mike and Jump put on their Kevlar vests before heading to the area. Once they arrived they saw a group of young men blocking the road with their beat up cars. They were huddled around the hood of a big green Buick LeSabre that would have looked good about two decades ago. Mike blew his siren once and used the megaphone in his car to instruct them to put their hands where he could see them. Once he stopped the car both Mike and Jump got out but stayed behind their doors. Mike continued to tell the guys to back up to the sound of his voice and then kneel with their hands over their heads. Most of the hoodlums complied knowing nothing would come of the impromptu search but one guy all of a sudden took off running toward the back of a nearby house.

Mike asked Jump as he was unbuckling his seatbelt: "You got this?"

"Of course I do and I have already radioed for backup. You go."

Mike quickly got out of the car and started after the guy. The runner wasn't fast, probably due to the smoke in his lungs and Mike was quickly gaining on him and yelling for him to stop. The young druggie turned to look at Mike and popped something into his mouth. Mike was close enough to tackle him all the while telling him to spit it out.

"Come on, chuck it!" Mike was getting irritated with the guy. He put his knee on the guy's back and pulled out his handcuffs.

"No man, I'm not going back in." Mike could see the guy was scared and obviously high on something.

As Mike snapped the handcuffs in place he questioned the guy. "What's your name?"

"Pete."

"Well Pete. Running is never good especially when you try to out run someone who is clearly in better shape than you." Pete was huffing and seemed to be having trouble catching his breath. His pupils were dilated and he was beginning to shake. "What did you put in your mouth?"

"None of your business," Pete said. Mike roughly pulled Pete to his feet and told him to start walking.

"Man, I got rights! You can't just handcuff me. Get these things off and then you can just take yourself away and drive that sorry cop car out of here. You ain't welcome in case you didn't notice," Pete said.

Mike gave Pete a shove to get him moving toward the squad car. Pete didn't want to cooperate so Mike was forced to grab Pete's wrists and continue to push him along.

As they approached the car Mike said, "Jump, get that back door." But just as he said that Pete went limp and fell to the ground and began shaking uncontrollably. "What the heck?" Mike stumbled over Pete and became alarmed at his behavior.

Jump, who had all of the guys cuffed with zip ties and sitting on the curb, said: "I think you've got one about to OD there."

Mike used the radio on his collar to call for EMS. Pete was still shaking and turning redder by the second. The good thing about city neighborhoods is the proximity to emergency services. EMS sirens could already be heard in the distance.

Mike moved any big rocks and debris out of the way and just stood close to Pete. "You guys need to tell us what he's on so we can help him."

"Man ain't none of your business what a dude chooses to put in his own body." This was said by a white guy in his mid-twenties. He looked familiar to Mike. Probably was a repeat rider in his squad car.

"I don't care what you think, loser. Answer the man." Jump gave the guy a kick on the soles of his shoes to drive home the point.

"I ain't telling you shit."

"Well, you assholes will probably all be singing by the time we get you charged." Jump was collecting all of their wallets and other items located in their pockets. He was coming up with a treasure trove of drugs, cell phones, and loose cash. These guys would be living at tax payer expense for the foreseeable future. Jump was only too glad to escort them there.

Mike was watching Pete as he continued to shake. The shaking seemed to be subsiding a little but he didn't know if that as a good thing or not. Pete's face was covered in dirt that was stuck to the saliva falling out of his mouth. A raw spot on his face had opened up and was bleeding and was also becoming caked with dirt and blood.

The EMS pulled up and two technicians exited the vehicle, ran to the back of the truck and grabbed a stretcher and a large black pack and then ran to Pete.

One of them asked: "What do you know about the patient?" He proceeded to take readings on Pete and make sure his air passage way was clear. As he began getting blood pressure and pulse readings he called them out loud. All Mike knew was they were all high.

Mike responded, "He swallowed a stash of something. He was a runner when we pulled up to the drug deal. I imagine he's got some form of meth in him besides whatever he swallowed."

The second EMT pulled out a syringe and stuck it in Pete's arm. "This is naloxone. It should help him breathe easier. If he's got any meth or oxycodone in him his breathing has been compromised. This'll help."

The other technician was keeping a running dialogue with someone on the other end of his radio, probably an emergency room doctor. He asked, "You said he swallowed something?"

"Yes, most likely some crystal meth. It's what my partner found on some of the other guys."

"Ok, we'll have to take him in and see what the doc can do about the stomach contents." They began loading Pete on the stretcher and grabbed their bag and ran back to the bus. Everything happened in a matter of minutes. Pete was on his way to the hospital and after Jump and Mike got the other druggies booked they would swing by the hospital to check on Pete.

Mike radioed in their progress and for someone to meet the ambulance at Regional Hospital and secure Pete. He was also under arrest even if he did overdose. Of course he had to survive it first and it appeared it was questionable if he would. This was just the beginning of what would turn out to be a long night for Mike and Jump.

Chapter 17
Lucky Sam

Sassy A's was doing a booming business and everyone was glad when the night dragged on because it meant more money all the way around. The dancers were bringing in the big bucks and the booze was flowing freely. Lucky Sam was grinning like the proverbial cat that swallowed the canary. Even the two Berts could tell he was happy.

"Boss, you sure look happy." Albert usually hesitated to ever speak directly to Lucky Sam but the smile on Lucky Sam's face invited a comment. Ever since the confiscation of the Flowers' meth lab, Lucky Sam had been racking in some extra bucks. People were addicted to their meth and paid whatever was required in order to get their next fix. It all made the businessman in Lucky Sam start thinking about how to grow that aspect of his business. If he could cook his own product, then he could get rid of the jokers he currently employed to bring him the speed. Meaning more profits for him. So he sent one of his loyal underlings that had some knowledge of cooking and got him to create a special mix of the cotton candy. The one requirement was the meth had to be green because Sam liked the color of money and this was going to bring him even more cash. Plus, the color would let everyone know who to go to get more of the stuff.

"Even your ugly mug can't make me upset tonight. I've got a new product that is moving and brining in some new revenue. I may even remodel a bit." Lucky Sam probably wouldn't remodel but he could dream. He liked his cash divided between being deposited in the bank and in his own personal safe in his office. That way he could monitor it and get his hands on some whenever he wanted. Tonight, Lucky Sam's drug mules had brought in the proceeds from the first sales of his homegrown crystal meth. He could tell it was going to be a cash cow for him.

"Get me the dishwasher." Lucky Sam had noticed Bud hadn't brought in his share of the money tonight and it was due. He needed to find out what was up with him.

Bert One went to get Bud and hoped he'd put up a stink about it so Bert could punch him. Bert couldn't stand the skinny mule and wouldn't mind having to take care of him permanently.

"Yo, Dickhead! The Boss wants you now." Bert stood in the door with his arms crossed. He knew his size intimidated the dishwasher so he liked to tower over the little guy whenever he could.

Bud jumped when Bert called out for him which made Bert One howl with laughter.

Bud yelled, "Asshole! Some of us have real jobs and don't get the luxury of sneaking around."

"I work for the Boss and he said to get you. I'm happy to carry you if you need assistance."

"I've got to get these dishes cleaned for the next shift. Hey, let go of me." Bert had come over and grabbed Bud around the waist and started physically carrying him to the Boss's office.

"I'm taking your scrawny white ass to the Boss so just shut up." Bert carried Bud all the way down the hall and into the office.

Lucky Sam looked up at the commotion. "Put him down Bert and go back up front."

Bert left the room a little pissed that he didn't get to stay and hear why the Boss wanted Bud. He hoped it was bad and he hoped the Boss would tell him to give Bud some special one-on-one time later.

Lucky Sam got up from his desk, walked over to the door, closed it, and turned to Bud. "You got my cash?"

Bud was beginning to get nervous. He kept wringing his hands with his apron. "I've got half of it."

"What? Since when did I ever take half of a payment? I'm beginning to think I need to let Bert teach you some respect."

"No Boss! I'll get it tonight and give it to you tomorrow. I know the stuff is bad and I didn't' want to lose any regular customers to it."

"That ain't for you to decide. But just because I am in a good mood because my other dealers brought in ALL of their cash and orders for more, I'll give you 24 hours to get me your share. There'll be a late fee of course. You don't get your cut this time. Instead you get to keep your life. Now get back to work before I get mad and change my mind." Lucky Sam walked to his desk and Bud made a quick retreat out of the room.

Back in the kitchen Bud was still shaking. He knew that was close and he was going to have to move the product. He had a bad feeling about Lucky Sam's meth. It was going to be dangerous to his customers. Maybe it was time to turn in Lucky Sam too. Bud continued to wash the dishes while he thought about what he needed to do after his shift ended.

Chapter 18
Bud

It was late when Bud finally cruised around his neighborhood looking for any of his regulars who needed a fix. He would go ahead and sell the meth and just hope nothing bad happened. Then he'd give the money to Lucky Sam and tell the police where he got the drugs.

He spotted a couple of young guys who were new to his turf. *I bet they'd like some of this stuff,* Bud thought. "Hey guys!"

The two wanna-be thugs turned to see who called out to them. When they saw it was Bud they smiled and slowly strutted over to Bud. "What's shaking man?" The fellow who asked barely looked twenty and already his face was marked with the acne that habitual drug use brings. His buddy was maybe a year older and when he smiled at Bud his teeth, or lack thereof, gave credence to the fact he was an addict and probably a very serious one too. His teeth were already rotting and the ones he had left were yellowed and looked diseased. Obviously these two loved their addictions more than their health. Well, it was none of Bud's concern. He just needed the proceeds from the sale to give to Lucky Sam.

"Hey dudes. I got some new stuff and you two are just the ones to give it a try and spread the word."

"What you got?" the one with no teeth asked.

"This is a potent mix that will make you feel like you're swimming in sunshine as soon as you take it." Bud was a good salesman when it came to pushing his stash.

"Tell me more." The younger of the two kept shifting from foot to foot.

"I tell you what I'm gonna do. I will let one of you have a sample and you can tell the other how good it is and then I'll sell you what I got for twenty bucks a pop."

"I don't know, man. That seems steep for something I ain't never heard of."

"Man, it's just a new product. That's why I'm giving you a free sample. Soon everyone'll know about it and the price will skyrocket. I'm just trying to help some of my faithful customers. You guys are on the ground floor of a new drug. If it takes off I can even let you guys in on some of the sales." Bud had no plans to do that but he knew he needed to get the guys to purchase Lucky Sam's Green Speed. Damn, he hated the stupid name. Hopefully tonight he could sell it all and be done with it. Then he could head home and get some sleep.

"What's it called?" The fidgety one seemed interested in trying something new. Probably because his usual fix wasn't getting him quite the same good feeling anymore.

"Lucky Sam's Green Speed because it'll be all systems go and make you feel like you're a new person, like you can do anything." Bud had no idea how it really made you feel but these two idiots wouldn't either.

"Let me have the free stuff and Tiny here will pay ya' for his share." Tiny was the one with no teeth and was also about six feet five inches tall and skinny as a rail. His buddy was only about five eleven and carried a gut on his shorter frame. Bud figured the shorter one could handle the drug better so he agreed to let him have the free sample. Bud pulled out a pair of gloves he took from Sassy A's kitchen and put them on.

"Why you putting on gloves?" Tiny asked.

"I just want to keep the product pure for you and not taint the flavor. I had to wash dishes earlier and my hands smell like fish." They didn't but Bud didn't want to touch the stuff. He had a bad feeling about it and didn't want deal with it let alone touch it.

"What do I do with it?" asked Tiny's friend.

"Swallow it," Bud said as he held out the rock for the human guinea pig.

"Take it, Shrimp, and tell me how you feel like sunshine is all over you, ya' know, like the man said."

The one called Shrimp took the pellet and placed it in his mouth. He closed his eyes and let the substance dissolve. "Wow, that is psychedelic! I feel so good."

Shrimp started walking around and leaned against a tree. He was clearly enjoying his high and Bud was glad to see he hadn't keeled over and died as soon as he took it.

"Let me have some!" Tiny was eager to reach the same high as Shrimp.

"Give me twenty bucks first." Tiny pulled out a wadded up twenty and handed it to Bud. Bud, who still had his gloves on, handed a rock to Tiny who immediately popped it in his mouth.

"Niiiiccceee." Tiny also walked over to the tree where his buddy was and leaned against it. The two addicts seemed like they were going to be able to handle the potent and potentially lethal homemade meth.

"You guys want one for the road? I need to go sell this before it expires. It needs to be sold pretty quick to keep it pure." Again, Bud didn't know anything about the so called shelf life of the drug but he wanted it gone and he knew if it was in demand it would go quicker.

Silent Rage

"I'll take another hit for later." Shrimp reached in his pocket and pulled out an equally dirty and wadded twenty. Bud gave him a rock and then got in his car to find more suckers for the drug. Shrimp and Tiny gave Bud a false sense of ease that anything bad was going to happen with selling this drug. Maybe he worried for nothing, he thought as he revved his motor and drove off leaving the two addicts in their own green haze of sunshiny happiness.

Chapter 19
Mike

Johnny's Burgers and Dogs was a town landmark. It was first established in 1931 as a resource for people to get a meal at a low cost and quite often at no cost. Johnny Williams was one of the lucky ones during the Great Depression. He ran a small grocery store and fully believed the tough times were merely a setback and better times were coming. Because human beings needed food and Johnny priced things fairly, he was actually doing well financially. He also had great success selling a few other miscellaneous items like the Emerson Bedroom Radio. It sold for just under ten bucks and he couldn't keep enough of them in stock. It seems even in desperate times folks liked to listen to the news and music that came out of the wood-grained boxes. It helped them to briefly forget their troubles and be entertained by programs such as "The Detective Story Magazine Hour" or "Hollywood Hotel." That's why Johnny always kept a radio on at work.

Johnny had a compassionate heart and when his neighbors were going hungry he took all of his soon to expire meats and produce and served them up to anyone who needed it. He set up a grill and a picnic table behind the grocery store and spread the word he had extra food. To those who came all he asked was for anyone who could to leave some spare change in the jar on the table. If you couldn't pay, no problem, you can always pay when times were better. Needless to say he was loved and his impromptu deli grew rapidly. Soon he needed to get a second grill and some help and before long he parked a silver trailer on the lot and worked right out of it. Johnny's

Burgers and Dogs grew so fast Johnny sold his grocery store to a new company called A&P and concentrated solely on his food business. Johnny had one of the earliest fast food restaurants and soon opened up more stores in other cities. He kept a small portion of his food to donate to homeless shelters and he always let a poor hungry person grab a free meal. Today the original site is still home to Johnny's Burgers and Dogs and is a favorite of local police officers who need a good meal cheap and fast. Johnny has long gone on to serve burgers to anyone hungry in heaven and his great-grandson, Johnny IV lovingly called Big Red, is now the man behind the grill. He has a soft spot for cops and only charges them a dollar no matter what they order. Most cops leave a good tip in the jar still located on the picnic table. Same jar. Same table. Some things are simply too good to change.

"Hey Big Red! How about a double cheeseburger for me and three loaded dogs for my man Jump and a couple of orders of fries?" Mike greeted the tall red-headed man and leaned on the counter at the window where orders were placed.

"What's up Mike? Things going smoothly?" Big Red threw a burger on the grill with his right hand and simultaneously grabbed a hot dog with the tongs in his left hand. Big Red weighed about 300 pounds easily and had heart to match. Although when he was a kid he wanted to be a police officer, as he grew older and spent summers working at the restaurant, he came to realize his future was in meat. When he graduated high school he started working full time and never looked back. That was ten years ago.

"Same ole, same ole." Mike replied. "We've been busy with some drug deals going on in the area. You ever see anything shady happening at your tables?"

"Nah and if I did I'd just chase 'em down with the Babe here and run 'em off!" the Babe was a wooden baseball bat his grandfather obtained to run off wayward youth back in the '50s.

"Well, you ever have any trouble you give us a call, and let us do our job."

"Mmm, mmmm, mmmmm! Man I smell me some good dogs!" Jump walked up to the trailer and leaned against the window beside Mike. He handed a bottle of water to Mike and took a long drink himself. They kept a case of the stuff in their car. "I can smell them all the way down the street." Jump had stayed in the patrol car to call his wife while Mike placed their order and now he was ready to eat.

"Everything ok at home?" Mike asked.

"Yeah, she just likes to hear her sexy man's voice frequently throughout the day." Jump winked at Mike. In reality his wife did like to hear his voice periodically but it was to make sure he was still alive and well. She did not want to be the wife greeting a chaplain at the door and felt as long as Jump called in frequently he would be safe.

"Here's your order gentlemen." Big Red handed two large bags to the officers.

Mike asked, "How much we owe ya?"

"For my two favorite officers, same as always, nada."

"You know we can't do that. It's an ethical violation." Jump may know his drug lingo but Mike knew his police protocol. In his department it was considered a police ethics violation to accept free food and beverages from local merchants. This came about as a result of a lawsuit filed against the city several years ago. It seemed a young officer developed a crush on a store owner's daughter. The cop would find any number of reasons to stop by the small hardware shop which also carried a vast array of snack foods. The girl's father was happy to have a member of law enforcement stopping by frequently so he never let the young officer pay for his snacks.

Soon word got out about the generosity of the owner and before long just about every police officer in the station dropped in for a free snack. As luck would have it the store got robbed one day. The owner called 911 expecting one of his many friends to rush to his aid and save his store. That was not the case. It happened to be a busy night for crime and the nearest available unit didn't arrive for over 30 minutes. In the meantime, the thief stole all the money along with many valuable items and beat up the owner leaving him with a broken rib and nose along with thousands of dollars of damage and lost merchandise. The angry man filed a lawsuit against the city. The most damaging aspect of the case was the collection of photos of various police officers in essence stealing his food. The city quietly settled. The business dried up. The owner moved away and the love affair never had a chance after the robbery.

Now the police officers have to sign an ethical code and suffer dire consequences if they violate it.

"So just pay the usual dollar per item and know I appreciate ya," said Big Red. Mike handed him the seven dollars covering the burger, fries, and hot dogs and secretly placed a ten in the jar.

The two officers found an empty picnic table and settled down to eat.

"You going house hunting this week?" Jump was aware Mike was planning to buy a house and then propose to Libby when he carried her over the threshold the first time.

"Yep. It's all lined up. The realtor's got several to look at and Libby is going with me to give the final say so."

"Man, that's good you're taking her 'cause if you just picked out the house on your own you'd never hear the end of it, and you'd end up selling sooner rather than later." Jump had been married close to two decades and often chose to deliver his marital advice to Mike. Not that Mike minded at all. He liked to hear about successful marriages especially in the day and age of quickie divorces. It seemed no one stayed committed to each other "til death do us part" anymore.

Just as the two hungry men took a healthy bite of their meals the radio burst to life calling them to a possible drug deal. Knowing that every second counted when it came to trying to catch a deal in progress, they grabbed their food and ran to the car. Once they were each buckled in they sped off. The address the dispatcher gave them happened to be in the same area as the home of their latest confidential informant. In the ten days since he signed the agreement, Mike and Jump's CI, Bud, hadn't delivered any worthwhile information.

"That's Bud's neighborhood. Maybe tonight's the night Bud will come through for us," Jump stated.

Chapter 20
Mike

When the officers arrived on the scene there was a group of young men huddled in a circle. As the patrol car's headlights swept the area the gang split and ran. Mike and Jump immediately parked the car and gave chase to the guys. Jump quickly overtook a heavy set boy who couldn't be more than sixteen. Mike was pursuing a more agile guy and the two were running in between the trailers in the area. Mike caught a glimpse of a third guy running into an old abandoned and darkened trailer. He pulled his gun out and ran down a different alley and actually got ahead of the young drug user he was chasing. Mike figured he was heading for the same trailer the other guy hid in and his assumption paid off. Mike was waiting on the guy at the door. The teen ran straight into the waiting arms and handcuffs of Mike who then cuffed him to a piece of metal on the trailer that made a convenient loop for Mike to use. Calling for backup Mike then cautiously entered the darkened trailer.

With his police-issued gun leading the way Mike kicked the door to the unit open and started to enter. Sirens could be heard in the distance and Mike was sure they were headed his way. Once inside the old building Mike gave his eyes a chance to adjust to the dark. He noticed a rancid odor coming from somewhere further inside the trailer. It smelled like a bunch of dead animals had gotten trapped inside and died. It was very quiet in the trailer. As his eyes got used to the dark Mike could see an old orange and yellow plaid sofa pushed up against the wall opposite him. It was so threadbare the foam stuffing poking out of the holes in the fabric. The coffee table had seen better days as well. On top of the veneered table was the leftover paraphernalia of many drug parties. There were needles, baggies, cigarette butts and even an old Bunsen burner and some spoons which were blackened from heating over a flame to get the liquid fix some addicts craved. Prevailing over all of the drug trappings, however, was trash. The volume of debris scattered around the trailer was mind boggling. Alcohol bottles and beer cans covered just about every possible surface and floor space in the mobile home. The junk was the dominate feature of this place that long ago was someone's home.

Mike scanned the room and didn't see the druggie who ran in the place. He slowly entered further into the space all the while looking for and expecting someone to jump out at him. That's when he felt as well as saw a shadow in what must be the master bedroom. Mike tensed up and once again let his Glock lead the way.

"Hey man. Put that piece away. It's just me." The shadow turned out to be Bud the CI.

"You're lucky I didn't shoot you. What are you doing?" Mike was irritated with Bud for many reasons. He had not done anything to help the police try to stop some of the drug trafficking in the area and it looked like he was still the main dealer.

"I figured once The Man was called you'd be the one to show up. So I got to thinkin' now was the time to show you the lowdown of the area and I had to run so as I wouldn't look guilty. Know what I'm sayin'?"

As a matter of fact, Mike did understand what Bud was saying. The life of a drug addict is a short one anyway and if the others know you were a snitch then your life is all but over. The next conversation a discovered snitch had was the one his body told the coroner. "OK, so why am I in here?" Mike asked.

"There's a new drug hitting the streets and it's bad. It can kill ya' if ya' just touch the stuff. My supplier is wantin' me to move it and I ain't wantin to be around it. Know what I'm sayin?"

"Keep going."

"It's called Green Speed. I just call it Green cause I hate the name but it's a mixture of some bad shit," Bud explained.

It never ceased to amaze Mike how drug dealers just randomly mixed ingredients in the hope of creating a new product and therefore new junkies. They often made their lethal mixtures in rolling meth labs. These moving laboratories are on the rise since the money is so good in methamphetamine production. Some guy decides he is going to cook some meth so he buys something with wheels like an old recreational vehicle. He then finds an isolated place to cook his meth and hopefully not blow himself up in the process. That's usually how law enforcement found the labs though, blown apart and burned up along with whoever was inside cooking. Mike couldn't understand why anyone would want to even sample something created by a bunch of criminals. Now it looks like there's a new guy getting in on the meth business.

Bud proceeded to inform Mike of some of the drug deals going on in the neighborhood. Believe it or not, Bud was actually a concerned dealer. He wanted to keep his customer base bringing in his money and he needed them alive for that. Mixing meth and speed was already notorious and Bud didn't want to get started with the lethal cocktail. Because he was so afraid of Lucky Sam, Bud was hesitant to tell Mike anything. But Lucky Sam's Green Speed literally had Bud scared to death so he was willing to help Mike get the supplier off the street. There was always a way to find drugs to sell so Bud wasn't worried about not having any merchandise. In order to get the police to come, Bud had set-up a deal in front of an old lady's mobile home. She was about the only resident of the neighborhood who wasn't involved in some seedy aspect of life. Bud was certain she would call 911 and he was right. She did indeed see the transaction and called for the police to come quickly.

"So tell me who the dealer is. As our CI you're supposed to give us info we can actually use and so far you haven't. If we can get this guy, then we can keep you out of jail. You don't help us get him and the next time we're called out here you'll be away for life." Mike was irritated with the little info Bud had sent his way and wasn't willing to go easy on him at this point.

"The guy goes by Lucky Sam. When he delivers my goods and collects his money he sends his two heavies. They're called Bert. Both of 'em. I think they're brothers or something. I mean real brothers as in they got the same mother. They don't say much but they are two mean SOB's. I once saw one of 'em take a knife and slit a guy across the face 'cause he was short fifty bucks. Guy ended up with 25 stitches and now he looks like the Joker from Batman.

"Lucky Sam is a mean mother. The first time I met him was back when I was setting up my business. He comes out in a big black SUV with tinted windows and a driver. Lucky Sam gets out of the back and walks up to me.

He was smoking a big stogie and blew that smelly shit all in my face. I was afraid to blink 'cause the man is solid muscle. He works out all the time and when he ain't at the gym he's at his strip club down on Union. About that time this other black SUV pulls up and the Berts get out with a skinny white chick. She's screaming and crying and sayin' she didn't mean to keep the money. Lucky Sam just stays all calm and everything and walks up to her and gets up in her face. He pulls out a S&W and puts it right against her head. She wets herself and he takes the gun and shoots her in the crotch. She falls down and he shoots one of her tits off. I ain't never seen anything like it. The boob just flies away. Of course she's screaming and really crying now and that's when I notice one of the Berts is videoing the whole thing right on his phone and he's smiling too. Then Lucky Sam tells the other Bert to finish her. Bert one keeps right on recording and when the bitch is dead Lucky Sam tells Bert two to send the video to the club. I heard later that he showed the footage to his girls and just said "don't ever cheat me" and since then I don't think anyone ever has."

Mike was horrified about the murder of the girl. He could also understand why Bud was afraid of the dealer. Mike was familiar with the club and knew a man named Sam Dawkins owned it. Now he was seeing a connection to the drug trafficking in the area. Sam usually managed to keep himself removed from any unlawful acts which was why he was still in business. Vice had long suspected him but didn't have enough to make an arrest. Mike was glad he was going to have some news to share with Raymond. Maybe they could finally get the guy and put him away for good.

"One more question. Does Lucky Sam always use his two heavies to get the product to you?" Mike was trying to formulate a plan in his mind for taking down Sam.

"Most of the time he uses his two goons but I wash dishes at his club and he sometimes gives me product there. He don't like to though, 'cause he wants to keep his hands clean, if ya' know what I mean." Bud supplied the additional information but was beginning to get worried about his new role as an informant. "I need to get out of here. That's all the info I got now."

Mike said, "OK, so hang on a second I want to write some notes. You need a perp walk?"

"I need the walk and I need you rough me up a bit, if ya' don't mind."

Mike was happy to oblige and hit Bud right across the cheekbone before he knew what was coming.

"Damn! I mean like a scratch or somethin'. I didn't want you ruinin'' my face." Bud was gingerly holding his hand over his right eye and cheekbone. It was already swelling up and tuning a deep red. He was going to have quite a shiner which will just give him some credence in the neighborhood to talk about police brutality.

"Nothing could mess up your ugly mug. I probably improved it. Maybe now you can get a girl without paying for one." Mike handcuffed Bud and then pushed him out of the trailer and toward the patrol car.

After Mike delivered Bud to the station for his mock processing, he finished up his paperwork and took off for the day. He had the next two days off and he was going to spend most of that time with Libby. He was hopeful one of the houses would fit his budget and her dreams and they could begin the official plans of starting a life together.

All in all, it was a productive night and Mike and Jump talked about how they were going to try and catch Lucky Sam. It wouldn't be easy.

Chapter 21
Libby

The doorbell rang in Libby's third floor apartment. Giving herself a quick glance in the mirror she went to open the door.

"Hi, Mike!"

"Hi, yourself," Mike said as he pulled Libby into a warm embrace. He nuzzled her neck and commented on how good she smelled. Libby melted into his arms enjoying the attention.

"We aren't going to get much accomplished if you keep at this," Libby said with a smile in her voice.

"Maybe I like this more than going to look at houses."

Libby giggled and reminded him they had discussed that he wanted to buy a house and fix it up for her before they got married and she moved in. Once she was living there he didn't want his time taken up with renovations. His budget would only allow for so much and they agreed maybe he should buy a "fixer upper" to save money and get more house for the dollar. Mike wanted to make sure she was in on choosing the house, so on their first simultaneous day off they made arrangements to look at several houses with a realtor.

Libby gave Mike one last lingering kiss and then gently disentangled herself. "Let's go and don't forget I want a biscuit and a coffee first."

"Well, then let's get you fed before you turn into a hungry monster on me." Mike teased her knowing she was not generally a morning person and especially not one before at least two strong cups of coffee. Mike held the door for Libby and then took her keys to lock the door.

They went down three flights of stairs and Libby saw Mike was driving his pride and joy, a BritishTR6. It was a 1974 tan and black model that needed some repairs and he was able to talk the owner into letting him have it for four thousand dollars. It was a good find and Mike had lovingly restored it and now took it out on special occasions. His time with Libby was always something he treasured, especially when he didn't have to drive his police issued black and white.

"The Queen is looking might spiffy today." Libby loved the car and called it the Queen since it was a British model. Even Mike now referred to the car by the nickname.

"She's all spit-shined for you." Mike held the door open and then walked to his side and jumped over the door to slide into the driver's seat. Libby laughed at him and the two drove off for breakfast.

A few hours later and after seeing many houses that just weren't suitable even if the price was right, the realtor led them to a quaint neighborhood that had lots of well-kept mid-sized homes. The house they pulled up to was a one-story ranch and other than having a somewhat overgrown yard, appeared to be very nice. It was a red brick house with black shutters and a red front door. It gave the impression of a very traditional and colonial feel about it before even taking the first step inside.

Libby said as much to the realtor: "This looks very nice but above our price point."

"Normally you would be right. This home, however, belonged to a young doctor who got recruited by a hospital from another state and he just wants to sell the house and be done with it. The house is priced to sell and is sold as is. That means other than the major issues such as plumbing, you would assume any of the repairs needed to get the house up to date."

Jill Westmueller was a no nonsense realtor which is precisely why Libby chose her after talking to several potential realtors. Jill was in her mid-forties and had been selling real estate for close to two decades. She had lots of experience and was known for being a bulldog when it came to looking out for her clients. As first time buyers, it was important to Mike and Libby to have someone who was their advocate guide them through the process. Both Mike and Libby had heard horror stories about last minute issues causing a sale to fall through. Neither of them wanted that to happen and Jill seemed like a perfect fit for them.

Jill continued giving them the details about the house as she entered her realtor code in the lockbox to retrieve the key and open the door. "Let me tell you a little about the house before we go in. It is 15 years old and the original owners had a young and growing family. They outgrew the size of the house when they had their sixth child."

"Good gosh, I guess they did." This from Mike who was letting Libby do most of the talking with the realtor. "How many bedrooms?"

"The house has three bedrooms and two full baths. The décor is dated and the floors need to be refinished or replaced. The doctor who bought the house figured he would have time on the weekends to remodel but his time just didn't allow for that. So be prepared for some nursery themes and lots of beige and vinyl because that was all the rage when this home was built." Jill opened the door and motioned for Libby and Mike to proceed her.

The outside of the house may have been somewhat stately in appearance but the inside was another story. The front entry way was a nice size but had a faded and worn faux rock floor. The next room to enter was a great room followed by a large eat-in kitchen. The kitchen floor was also in vinyl and had the appearance of marble squares forming a pattern and in each corner was a blue diamond. The cabinets seemed to be in decent shape and were a nice shade of white. Off the kitchen was a huge laundry room which also doubled as a pantry. The bedrooms were at the opposite end of the house and were covered with wall to wall carpet in a very dingy brown. One bedroom was a bright pink and had clouds painted in random places on the wall. The other bedroom was blue and had truck decals across the top of the walls as a sort of border.

Libby commented: "Clearly they had a boy's room and a girl's room. I can only imagine what the master is like."

"You might be pleasantly surprised," Jill said.

They entered into the master bedroom and noticed the wall of windows across the back which overlooked the patio area and a very nice backyard.

"Wow, what a view. You're right, this is a pleasant surprise." Libby walked over to the windows and looked at the sizable lawn.

The realtor commented, "There is a lot of room out back for a swing set and sandbox." She smiled as she said it and Libby and Mike just grinned. They did plan to have a family somewhere down the road.

"This does seem nice but I noticed you've kept the price from us," Mike said as he moved to look in the master bath. The bathroom had a double sink and a shower tub combo along with a small linen closet. It was not a large space but definitely adequate.

"I have the price right here," Jill said as she handed the brochure on the house to Mike. She continued, "I did save the best house for last. This one won't last long and I do not want to pressure you by any means, but you may want to make an offer fairly soon if you decide on this home."

Mike opened the folder and looked at the price. While the realtor thought it was a steal it was slightly over Mike's budget. He looked at Libby to give her the agreed upon signal that a house wouldn't work but when he saw her face he couldn't bring himself to tell her no. He would just have to find a way to come up with the extra cash needed for the down payment.

Libby was already imagining herself living in this house and said to Mike, "I love it! I know it needs work but it has great bones. But if you want to discuss it before you make an offer we can always call Jill later."

Mike saw the look on Libby's face and knew he was going to buy this house. However, he did not want to appear too eager and so he told the realtor he did want to discuss it a bit and maybe he could call her later in the day.

Since they had driven separately from the realtor Mike and Libby said they would head to a coffee shop and talk about things and he would get in touch with Jill shortly.

"Oh Mike, I can just see us having dinners there and holidays. I can already see how to arrange the furniture."

Libby was excited about the future with Mike in the home. "What do you think?"

"I like it and if you do too then that's the one we'll get. I just didn't want to appear too eager and I want to offer lower than the asking price even though it is fair. You never know, the guy may be willing to take some off and that is only more cash for me to use in the updates."

The two went to eat a late lunch at a local deli and discuss the details of the purchase of the house. After they ate and talked, Mike put in a call to the realtor.

"Good afternoon. Jill Westmueller speaking."

"Hi, it's Mike O'Malley. I would like to make an offer on the house."

"Fantastic! Just to be clear we are talking about the three bedroom we saw last. Correct?"

"That's the one."

"I will get the offer drawn up and I can stop by your place later today and get your signature. Are you going with the asking price?" Mike could hear papers shuffling in the background as well as a computer booting up.

"Actually, no. I want to go a bit lower. I know the owner will probably counter but I would like to keep as much cash as I can since it does need updating." Mike explained.

"I understand the need for cash on hand but the owner is already cutting the price a good deal for a quick sale. I am not sure he would even counter because he has had multiple showings already. The house won't last long." Jill was being honest with Mike but he still wanted to try for a lower asking price.

"I understand all of that and if the house goes to someone else we will just keep looking. I want to try the lower price, though."

"OK, then what do you want to offer?" Jill asked.

They discussed the price and Jill promised to get the paperwork in order so they could send the offer to the owner soon.

Chapter 22
Libby

"So class, you can see the weapons the soldiers used changed a bit in the few short decades of early American history. The bayonet was no longer attached to the rifle but rather it was an individual knife used for protection and as an eating utensil for the soldiers." Libby   instructed her class in the changes in American society and technology during the time between the Revolutionary War and the Civil War. Her sixth grade class of 23 students included 15 boys and they all seemed to be budding young outdoorsmen. She knew most of the boys enjoyed camping with their Scout troops and had earned their Whittling Chip badge which allowed them to carry a pocketknife. The few who didn't belong to a troop still managed to find ways to be outside among nature. Of course, they were not allowed to carry pocketknives to school. Libby was thankful most of the boys understood the respect given to the weapon and therefore followed the rules because they didn't want to lose their badge and the privilege of carrying the small blade to Scout meetings.

"It's almost time for the bell so you may pack-up. Don't forget your writing assignment is due tomorrow. Take your favorite aspect of the changes in the lifestyles of Americans during this time between the wars and write about it. Start with your five "W's" and go from there. Spelling counts. You've known about this assignment all week so no late papers!"

The bell rang and Libby wished her students a good afternoon. She decided to enjoy the peace and quiet of the classroom and grade some papers before leaving for the day. No sooner had she gotten started when she heard a knock at her door followed by the entrance of a woman who could only be referred to as a cyclone waiting to happen. Esmeralda Cynthia La Pluma, lovingly called Essie by friends, family, and colleagues, burst into the room carrying a stack of papers. She wore a bright yellow flowy dress adorned with several necklaces sporting multiple chains and beads on each one causing her to play a sort of melody as she walked. Her bright red hair was piled high on top of her head and held in place by at least three paint brushes that Libby could see. Her feet were encased in ridiculously high bright red heels. Libby didn't know how she could teach in those things all day let alone walk in them. Essie was a student favorite because she was the art teacher and felt every student was a budding genius and displayed all their artwork around the school. When a student saw his or her creation proudly displayed on the hall walls, it made the student stand a bit taller and feel a bit prouder. Libby was just as fond of Essie and the two teachers often grabbed a quick coffee or bite to eat after work.

"I am simply baffled and at my wits end with this student's work!" Essie didn't bother with niceties such as how was your day but rather jumped right into whatever was currently on her mind and thought everyone else was on the same page mentally. Libby took a second to attempt to figure out which student was giving her grief. It must be one of hers since Essie came to her classroom.

Essie was a true redhead and had a few freckles spread across her nose and cheeks. She hated them but they really gave her an all-American kind of beauty. Those freckles were out in full force at the moment because Essie was clearly upset. Her green eyes were radiating anger. "This student repeatedly ignores my directions and draws what he wants to. He will use whatever technique I am currently talking about, which right now it happens to be Pointillism, and draw the same image over and over. I ask the students to draw their favorite objects by using nothing more than a series of dots to create the image. Most students choose something easy and well-known such as a beach ball or car. I even had one talented girl design a very detailed bikini. Well this student, and I want to see if you can guess who, keeps drawing knives!"

"Oh my gosh, it must be Russell Thomas." Libby put down her pen and the paper she was holding, all thoughts of grading papers gone. "You say he always draws knives on every assignment you give?"

"Not just draws them, they seem to consume him. Once I asked the students to draw a favorite object that someone had given them and, you guessed it, he drew a knife. I didn't give that much thought because I figured his dad had given him a pocketknife or something similar. Then when I asked students to draw their favorite gift they ever received and again he drew a knife. I wondered if it was the same drawing thinking maybe he didn't like art and just drew the same thing over and over so I compared his drawings. As you know I keep a folder on each student so it was easy to check. Every knife he drew was different and some were very elaborate. I questioned Russell about this and he just shrugged and said he liked to hunt. OK, that may be normal for his age and his family so I let it go. Then I got some more of his artwork and I thought maybe it was time to talk to the counselor."

"Hah! I am sure she was a wealth of information!" There was no love lost for Ms. Edwards where Libby was concerned.

"That's an understatement. She said 'boys will be boys' and it was all I could do not to throw the papers at her. Clearly she should've retired years ago. She doesn't even seem to like children so I have no idea how she ever ended up working with them." Essie's freckles were all but glowing now and her frustration was contagious. Libby found herself getting worked up as well.

"What do you want me to do?" asked Libby as she began stacking papers and neatening up her desk.

"Have you noticed any odd behavior or seen the type of artwork I am talking about on other students papers? Is it normal? Have you talked to his parents?" Essie was on a role and Libby was trying to get a word in edgewise. Even the beads swaying around her neck seemed to be picking up the tempo.

"Take a breath Essie!" Libby smiled as she said it. "Yes, as a matter of fact I have noticed his drawings on papers he turns in to me. And no, other students haven't drawn weapons of any sort on anything they've ever given to me. And finally, yes I have talked to his mom and I have even ridden out there to visit with her and get a feel for what kind of home life Russell has."

"What kind of reaction did his mom have?"

"She is hard to talk to on the phone and she works late hours so half the time when I've tried to call she's been sleeping and the other times some strange man answers. Since I was getting nowhere that way I decided to drive out to the home." Libby took a sip from the bottle of water she kept on her desk.

"What was that like?" Essie had a very inquisitive nature and was also good at listening as well as offering well-grounded advice when needed.

"A little scary." Libby proceeded to tell Essie about the strange guy hanging around the trailer. She also detailed the condition of the trailer itself and the half–clothed man that came to the door. She was able to convey her fear and her concerns while Essie listened attentively.

"I tell you what. Let's go grab a bite to eat and I'll ride out to his house with you. Maybe the two of us can get somewhere with this family." Essie volunteered to drive. "I'll meet you in the parking lot in 15 minutes." She left Libby's room to go get her purse and keys while Libby packed up her papers.

The two decided to eat at a local favorite where they had a decent variety to choose from. The diner was a throwback to the 1950's. It had Formica tables and red vinyl booths. It was a popular place and always had a waiting line. Libby and Essie entered the diner to the tingling of the bell attached to the door. After waiting in line at the counter they placed their orders and then searched for a table.

"Must be an early dinner rush. The place seems extra crowded for this time of day." Libby said.

"Over there in the corner. That couple looks like they're leaving." Essie said as she made her way to the booth and claimed it before anyone else could.

Libby slid into the booth. The redhead sat opposite Libby and took a sip of her soda. Just as the two got comfortable their pager vibrated signaling their meal was ready. Essie jumped up to go get the food. "Stay there, I've got this."

117

Essie placed their food trays on the table and said, "I have to admit I am anxious to see where Russell lives. I can't imagine living in a place like you've described. I have some serious concerns for the mental well-being of that boy."

"I hear you! But you need to tell me all about your date the other night!" Libby took a big bite of her grilled chicken sandwich and waited for Essie to finish chewing her own club sandwich.

Essie grinned and started glowing a lovely shade of red causing her freckles to intensify. The curse of the redhead only served to make Essie even more attractive. "Well, I had a great time."

"Go on! Don't leave me hanging!"

A couple of nights ago Essie had gone on a blind date with a fellow that Libby knew from college. Stan Kester was a local accountant who had just passed his CPA exam. A nice guy who was looking for an equally nice woman who was ready to settle down and eventually start a family. Stan was Mike's college roommate so naturally Libby had gotten to know him fairly well. Libby spent many hours in Mike's dorm and Stan was always polite to her. She was very fond of him and would love to see him find the right girl. She thought he and Essie would be a great match so she set the two up for a casual dinner date. Stan had sent her a brief text after the date with the simple words, "better than I thought" which of course left Libby craving the details of the date.

Essie was more forthcoming on those details. "Well, when I got to the restaurant I was nervous and had all kinds of fears of what the guy would look like, his clothes, and even his eating manners. Needless to say I was pleasantly surprised. No, shocked is a better word. The man is a hunk! Not only that, he treated me so sweetly and he didn't have any weird eating habits." Essie was well-known for having no tolerance for the idiosyncrasies of people's eating styles. At the top of her pet peeve list were people who blew their noses at the dinner table. The two friends finished up their meals and Libby got all the news about the date. Stan even asked Essie for another date this coming weekend. Libby was glad the evening was a success for both of her good friends.

They threw away their trash and stored the plates in the plastic bin left for dirty dishes and headed out the door. "You'll have to give me exact directions when we get closer. I sort of know where Spalding Avenue is but I am not sure of a couple of turns." Essie started her car and the two went off in hopes of finding out more about their mutual student.

Chapter 23
Mike

Mike and Jump were also heading to Spalding Avenue but for a completely different reason.

"This is the third time this week we've gotten a call for Spalding." Jump was finishing off a sub sandwich while he complained about the drug-ridden neighborhood.

"Bud gave us some good info last time. Since he told us about this meth and heroin concoction I've heard of 5 OD's already in the area. That stuff is bad and we need to get it off the streets as quick as possible." Mike was concerned the lethal concoction would soon hit the schools and the number of teen overdoses would skyrocket.

As the patrol car pulled onto the street they saw a crowd gathered around what appeared to be a small child lying on the road. Mike hit the siren briefly to get the people to move and parked the car. He and Jump ran over to the crowd. Both officers had their hands hovering over their guns and were on full alert ready for anything to happen. Just then a woman broke away from the circle of people and ran to the officers. "Please help my boy. He's only 11 and he's not breathing."

Mike radioed in for an ambulance and extra officers while Jump tended to the young boy and started administering CPR. The child was very small for his age and was already a gray color. Jump used his protective mouth piece and began blowing air into the child. Jump was very good at CPR but he could tell it was too late for the boy.

Mike asked the mother what happened.

"I don't know. One minute Caleb is out playing with his friends and the next they are yelling for me to help." The distraught mom looked older than her thirty or so years. She was rail thin and had stringy red hair. She was not a beauty and was clearly addicted to some drug herself, probably meth. That was a common drug in this area and she most likely sold her body just to get money to support her habit. Her addiction didn't stop her from loving her child and she was clearly worried.

Sirens could be heard getting closer and Jump did his best to keep some oxygen going into the boy and hopefully to his brain. He knew it was useless but he still went through the motions because sometimes miracles happened.

But not in this case. The EMS crew pronounced him dead and Mike called for the coroner to come to the scene. Mike and Jump took the mother into her unit and began the tedious process of determining just what happened to her little boy.

Both officers knew it was time to put a stop to the drug sales in this neighborhood. The death of a child from an overdose was simply something that should never happen anywhere. Surely even low life drug dealers cared about kids.

In fact, Lucky Sam was the dealer behind the sales in the area and he didn't care who bought and sold his merchandise as long as it moved and made him plenty of money. He never thought about the potential of his product getting into the hands of innocent children but even if he did he would have just figured people are going to buy what they want so it may as well be from him. Besides, in his eyes he was doing the community a service because he was a local guy which meant the money stayed in the neighborhood. His buyers could get to him easily and some didn't even have to drive to buy from his mules so maybe he had saved a life or two by keeping them off the road when they were high.

Chapter 24
Essie

The bright yellow Volkswagen Beetle with the flirty eyelashes on the front headlights seemed out of place amid the harsh glow of the multicolored first responder vehicles lining Spalding Avenue. Libby and Essie ceased talking to quietly take in the scene.

"Wonder what has happened?" Essie slowly maneuvered her car as close as she could get to the house Libby pointed out as belonging to Russell and his mom.

"It looks serious. I hope nothing has happened to Russell. I always worry that one day he is going to be hurt seriously from something going on at home." Libby was convinced Russell was the victim of child abuse but in just what form the abuse occurred she didn't have proof, only suspicions.

The punch bug continued its slow drive down the street. As the two teachers neared the scene a police officer stepped out and waved for them to stop. In the glare of the lights neither Libby nor Essie could tell who the person was. The patrolman stepped to the side of the car and it was then that Libby recognized Mike.

"Mike, what are you doing here?" asked Libby.

"The question is what are you doing here?" Mike gave a nod of hello to Essie.

"We're here to make a home visit to the student I've told you about. He lives just over there." Libby pointed to a mobile home that had seen better days about three decades ago.

Mike looked past the scene of the accident to the trailer Libby pointed toward. "What did you say his name was again?"

"Russell Thomas. Why? Has something happened to him?"

"No, this kid's name was Caleb." Mike said.

"Oh no! Not Caleb Wright? He's eleven but he's small for his age. Has a headful of dark hair and freckles across his nose. He's one of my art students." Essie described the boy with a catch in her throat.

Mike nodded his head and said, "That sounds about like him."

"Oh gosh, what happened to him?"

"It appears to be a drug-related incident and that's all I can say right now."

"Is he going to be ok?"

"No, I'm afraid not." Mike took a few more minutes to talk with them and then headed back to finish up his duties.

Essie was quiet after the news about her student. "I can't believe that sweet boy is gone," she said in a whisper.

"Me either. This drug problem for the kids in this neighborhood has gotten out of hand. It makes me all the more determined to step in and try to help Russell. What a bleak future he has right now." While both ladies discussed the plight of their students the ambulance made its way out of the neighborhood carrying the young boy on his last ride from home. "Should we go on home?"

Essie looked at Libby with wide eyes. "Are you crazy? No, maybe now is the time to get Russell's mom to actually listen, before he is the one getting carted off to the morgue." She started the car up and headed in a direction

124

where she could park it out of the way. Mike didn't notice the car parked behind some trees. He wasn't focused on Libby. He assumed she went home due to the tragedy.

Chapter 25
Libby

Libby knocked on the door of the trailer Russell called home. The door was opened by the same shirtless porcine-looking man who was there the last time Libby visited.

"You again! I told you to git and never come back."

"Good evening. We are looking for Loretta Thomas." Libby said.

"She ain't here." Wayne tried to close the door but Libby quickly grabbed it.

"Please. We just want to discuss Russell and some matters pertaining to his school work."

"I told you. That boy's a retard and he ain't gonna never go to college or nothing. You're wasting your time and mine. So get lost."

"Are you aware of the tragedy that just occurred?" Essie spoke up for the first time.

"Who the hell are you?"

"I'm Russell's art teacher and just now out on your street a young boy lost his life. Are you not even concerned about the dangers facing kids these days?" Essie asked.

"No. I survived and now it's their turn. I'm not asking again Now get out of here or I'll get my gun after you." Wayne crossed his arm over his fat gut and glared at Libby. Menace all but poured from his cold eyes.

Libby was fuming inside and said, "Technically you never asked, you just stated you wanted us to leave. Now, if you don't mind…" Libby was cut off in mid-sentence by Essie pulling her down the steps. "What are you doing?"

"I am getting you out of here before that mouth of yours gets us in serious trouble. It's obvious we will get nowhere with that pathetic excuse for a man back there."

Just as the two got within sight of Essie's car they saw a couple of darkly clothed figures run away. Both girls silently watched them disappear into the dark woods. Libby said what both were thinking, "Let's get out of here before they do something to us."

The two teachers walked to Essie's car and simultaneously noticed that something appeared off about the car. Essie realized what was wrong about a second before Libby did. Essie ran forward and put her hands on the side of her car and started simultaneously screaming and crying.

"Oh my gosh! Noooo!" Essie yelled as she stared at her car. Keyed into the side of her car were the words slut, bitch and FU. The yellow paint was now bleeding silver from the primer underneath. The windows were smashed in and there was also a dark mess which appeared to be mud but wreaked of something worse, smeared all over the outside of her car. Inside the car was no better. There were piles of what was some kind of excrement wiped over all the seats and a strong odor of urine poured out of the door when she opened it. What wasn't covered in waste was broken or ripped. Essie was in tears. Libby could only stand in silence with her arm around her friend trying to offer some comfort.

Libby gave Essie a hug and said she would call Mike and get him to come. They would handle this together. The good news was she had insurance. That didn't make Essie feel any better since she would be the one who had to deal with the hassle of having to get the car repaired.

Libby called Mike on her cellphone and he immediately radioed for help to get over there quickly just to protect the girls. He was back at the station house filling out his paperwork and it would take him several minutes to finish up and then head over to Spalding Avenue from the precinct. He didn't want Libby alone in that area any longer. He thought she was safe at home but he should've known she would find a way to talk to her student's family. She was a very stubborn woman and drove him nuts at times. Of course, her very feisty nature was one of the things he loved best about Libby. He got back to his paperwork so he could finish up and go be with her.

Chapter 26
Mike

Libby and Essie were sitting in the back of a patrol car when Mike arrived. There was already a crime scene crew going over the car. Mike went over to speak to the two friends and assure himself they were ok and then made his way to the damaged car.

"Man! This thing stinks!" Mike made his presence known.

One of the two officers processing the car spoke up. "I think it's human shit. At least some of it is. Of course we'll bag and tag it all. We've got a boatload of prints but I am betting they all belong to the two sitting in the car. I don't know what her insurance will say but I wouldn't want the car back if it were mine. The vandals pretty well messed up everything inside with either feces or urine. Totally disgusting!" The officer was the senior of the two and had seen many awful crime scenes in his day. He felt pity for the owner of the car. In his mind it was totaled. He just hoped the girl's insurance was good and treated her right.

"Clearly whoever did this was sending a message to them that they are not welcome in the neighborhood." The second officer processing the scene was busy taking photos of all the damage to the exterior of the once cheerful VW Bug. Mike knew Essie loved the car and was very proud of it since she had scrimped and saved in order to put a down payment on it. He would never understand why some people were so inconsiderate of the things that belonged to other people. Then again, it certainly kept him busy at work.

Mike went back to the patrol car to talk to the girls. He asked them if they had seen anyone and both told him about the darkly clad figures running away when they neared the car. Their description was the typical—average height, average size, and dark clothing that so many miscreants wear when committing a crime. Mike did not feel confident that the perpetrators would be caught. Barring a miracle unless they left fingerprints and were already in the system, they would probably get away with their crime and it would be up to Essie to make amends to herself. That stunk for her. Pun intended.

The patrol car left with Libby and Essie huddled up together in the back. It was taking them both home which, in Mike's mind, is where they should've been to begin with and then Essie's car would have been spared the defacing.

Chapter 27
Libby

Libby poured the fresh coffee beans into her burr grinder and set the coffee maker to grind and brew. She loved the aroma of the French dark roast and she knew it would keep her awake which she'd regret come five in the morning. It was a school night after all but she had some work to do before going to sleep. Besides, after the events of the evening she didn't think she would sleep much anyway so why not attack this assignment. Libby was taking graduate courses to obtain a masters in psychology which would serve a twofold purpose for her. First, she would get a raise at her teaching job, second, it would be one step closer to finally getting the PhD in criminology and profiling which was her ultimate goal. She loved crime. She also loved finding out what drove people to commit their often heinous acts. Libby believed people could be saved from a life of crime but that saving had to occur due to early intervention in the childhood of the future criminal. Libby heard the bubbling of the coffee maker signaling her brew was ready. She poured a big mug, added a splash of fat free creamer, and sat down at the table where her laptop waited.

Tonight's assignment was to discuss the treatment of youths in juvenile delinquent centers and if that treatment actually made a difference in their lives. She had done a lot of reading on this subject and it really boiled down to the old nature versus nurture argument. Were these young criminals born to be bad or had their environment molded them into lawbreakers. What treatment could really help at that point? She knew studies had been compiled on the brains of serial killers and many did have extra levels of rage hormones. However, just because a person had an extra bad temper didn't mean he was going to become a serial killer. These were the issues that fascinated Libby and she enjoyed her readings on this topic. She began to work on her essay and was writing about one young killer who was a very disturbing individual.

Evan Brady grew up never knowing his real mother. She abandoned him one day after dropping him off at her mother's house and then never returned to get him. She simply wanted to party and not have the responsibility of being a mother to a rambunctious two-year-old boy. She never was seen again by her son or her mother. Libby thought to herself, one has to wonder how this will turn out for the boy since the grandmother didn't do such a great job with her own child given she didn't seem to instill any sense of duty in the girl. However, his grandmother, known to all as Miss Mildred, did the best she could but she was frail and had to use a walker to get around. This meant she often had handymen in to do repairs and other odd jobs around the house. Her favorite one to use was the son of a nearby neighbor. What Miss Mildred didn't know was this man was a convicted pedophile and used every chance he could to go over to the woman's house. She thought he was wonderful and such a good person to want to help her when in reality he was sexually abusing little Evan and threatened to kill the old woman if Evan told on him.

Evan grew up thinking he was worthless and over time came to resent his grandmother. He didn't get to play sports like other boys because she couldn't get him there. Instead he had to tend to her which included being a waiter for the woman during her many Circle meetings. These were times when the neighborhood ladies would meet to discuss their most recent Bible study topics, but in reality the time was nothing more than a gossip session. Evan hated those days. He wanted to go play and be with other kids but he couldn't. This anger led him to rebel by committing petty crimes. He acted out in school, at least when he attended. Ultimately Evan was caught spying on women in dressing rooms and when the police came to question him they found stolen items in his pockets. Thus began a long period of being in and out of juvenile detention centers for Evan. He spent most of his preteen and about all of his teen years being raised by the guards in the prisons. Eventually he turned eighteen and they let him out. With nowhere to go he returned to his grandmother's home. She tried to enforce some guidelines for him but he was twice her size and easily intimated her. He quickly grew tired of her nagging and one day he simply hit her with a fireplace poker. The old woman's neck snapped when she fell out of her wheelchair onto the floor. Evan realized he had killed her and actually felt liberated. What he did next was what proved to Libby that nurture can create a criminal just as easily as nature can produce one at birth. Evan sawed off the old woman's head and placed it on the pillow in her bedroom. He would see it every night when he passed her room on the way to his own bedroom. It made him realize he was now free of any rules.

Evan had grown into a strong young man and had easily dismembered his grandmother and placed her body in large garbage bags. He put them in the big green trashcan by his backdoor and then on trash pickup day, which happened to be the next morning, he rolled the bin to the street and never saw her again. No one noticed the heavy bags since the truck had an automatic arm that picked up the containers and dumped them in the back. The driver just pushed a button which turned on the hydraulic door that compacted the trash. By the time the trash truck reached the dump there was a considerable amount of trash on top of Evan's bags and no one paid any attention to the big heap of fresh trash. It was the perfect crime. That is until a neighbor came to visit his grandmother. It seems that the elderly Viola and Evan's grandmother met a couple of times a week to have coffee and simply chat. When Viola asked Evan if she could come in and wait for his grandmother, Evan said no and told her his grandmother didn't want to see her again and she needed to go home. Fortunately for Viola she did just that. It saved her life because Evan was holding the poker behind his back ready to use it again if the neighbor didn't leave.

However, Viola didn't give up. She missed her friend and couldn't understand why she didn't call and tell her the reason why she no longer wanted to have coffee together. So Viola marched herself back over to her friend's house and once again knocked on the door. This time no one answered. Evan was out getting some groceries. Viola used the key on her key chain, she and Mildred had exchanged keys since they were both elderly and one never knew when someone would need to get in quickly, and entered the house. Immediately she noticed a sour smell. She called out for her friend while she was trying to locate the source of the odor. Eventually she went to the master bedroom where she discovered the rotting head of her old friend. She ran out of the house screaming and right into the arms of Evan. He simply picked up the frail woman and carried her inside. He got rid of the woman the same way he did his grandmother. He didn't keep her head though, since she didn't really mean anything to him. The trash came again and Viola was buried in the same dump not too far from her friend.

Viola had family who worried about her and grew concerned over her disappearance. It wasn't long before the police knocked on Evan's door and he was led away. He would eventually be deemed insane and forced to live out his years in a mental institution. Libby couldn't help but wonder if Evan would have resorted to this life of crime had his mother remained in the picture. Libby's mind also strayed to her student, Russell. She knew his mother loved him but his home life was far from desirable. Libby wasn't sure if Russell was getting the proper amount of nutrition and feared his only real meal was the one he ate in the lunchroom cafeteria. Besides her concerns over his food situation, Libby knew Russell didn't have many friends and was picked on by some of the bigger boys in the class. She knew Russell was absent frequently and was sure the bullying was part of the problem.

Russell was already missing far too many days of school and when he did come someone in the class always had some item go missing. Anything from a bag of lunch to money and even a handheld game device, which shouldn't have been at school to begin with, had been reported stolen. No one knew who was responsible but after studying juvenile criminals and the psyches within them, Libby was starting to suspect Russell. That just made her more determined to intervene and try to help Russell achieve something with his life other than living in prison at tax payer expense. Libby drained the last of the coffee pot and looked at the clock. She was shocked to see it was well after two in the morning. If she fell asleep this very second she would barely get three hours of sleep. She had morning bus duty at school and had to be there early. She shut off her computer and headed to bed to try and get some rest. All of her readings had her mind on overdrive and she knew it would be hard to simply close her eyes and sleep. Maybe she could use the time to come up with a plan for Russell.

Chapter 28
Russell

While Libby was reading about the misadventures of juvenile delinquents, Russell was busy patrolling the woods near his trailer. He liked to go exploring in the forests near his house. It was his way of escaping from home and in the thickets he could pretend he was a soldier and practice his guerilla warfare skills. He rubbed mud on his face and put leaves and sticks in his clothing and then hid behind bushes while he scouted out the area. He learned a lot about nature and the cycle of life by watching the animals native to the area give birth to their young, forage for food, and then return to the earth by decaying where they died. This actually fascinated him and when he went to the library he tried to find books to read about animal decomposition.

Tonight the woods seemed unusually active. Russell silently crept along trying to determine what was up. Before long he heard some small animals growling and followed their sound. About 20 yards ahead of him he saw two foxes pulling on something, maybe a stick. But Russell didn't know why they would be fighting over it. He quietly inched forward and that's when he saw the body lying on the ground. He gave an involuntary gasp and the foxes ran away. Russell hated to disturb nature but at least now he could go and investigate who that was on the forest floor.

He was very intent on the body that was supposed to be the dinner of the two foxes, so much so that he didn't see the one he tripped over. He fell down and caught himself roughly with his hands which sent a jarring pain up his right arm. He gently shook his hand and thought he most likely sprained his wrist. That wasn't a big deal. He knew how to take care of himself. He was now very interested in the second body in the ground.

Russell looked closely at both of the bodies he had discovered. He at first thought he should probably let somebody know about them, but he quickly dismissed the idea and instead sat on a nearby rock and just watched the insect activity that was evident on the bodies. He wished he had brought his backpack with him because he could make notes about the decaying process the two bodies were undergoing. It didn't matter, he just told himself, because he could make notes the next time he came out to see them. He knew he would be returning to see these two guys again.

Chapter 29
Mike

Mike entered the briefing room and took a seat next to Jump.

"Morning." Jump saluted Mike with a raised cup of coffee.

"You must've made a coffee run because I know you wouldn't drink that sludge they brew here." Mike stated.

"I am not putting anything of unknown origin into this temple and you know that coffee maker is a leftover from the last century and I ain't talking about the 1900's either."

"I think it's kind of rude of you to flaunt that in my face though, knowing I wouldn't have time to make my own coffee run."

"If you'd get your sorry ass out of bed just a little earlier you could get your own damn coffee. But since I know and love you so well," Jump reached over to the other side of his chair and pulled up a white bag, "I brought you one and a muffin so your whiny voice would shut up." Jump handed over the deli bag with a grin.

"You are the best partner ever, thanks!" Mike uncapped his coffee and took a long drink of the hot and fragrant brew.

"Alright, listen up." Captain Morgan made his way to the podium at the front of the room. All the officers immediately took a seat and ceased all talking. Captain Morgan was a no nonsense kind of guy. He ran his station efficiently with a tight rein on all the comings and goings. He was aware of the jokes that were made behind his back.

139

Silent Rage

It was because of his name. He was christened Jonathon Frank Morgan but everyone called him Jack from an early age. On his first day of his newly achieved rank of captain, Jack opened the office door to a room full of Captain Morgan rum. Each bottle had a black pirates hat resting on the bottle and the squad room broke into a chorus of yo, ho, ho's. Captain Jack merely smiled to himself then turned to the room and thanked them for the liquor. He assured them he would need it since he was over such a motley crew. This earned him immediate respect. The officers knew he could take a joke and yet remain in control of a situation.

"We have a situation developing out near Candie's Acres of Flowers. A Missy Flowers has reported her husband, Hank Flowers, missing." Captain Morgan pushed the clicker in his hand and a picture appeared on the screen in front of the room. "This is a photo of Hank from about a year ago. After Mrs. Flowers called, two officers were dispatched to drive out to the place to take the report. When they got there the entire Flowers family was waiting. All, that is, except for one Missy Flowers, the one who made the initial complaint. The matriarch of the family and mother of Hank assured us Hank was off on family business and it was a quick trip so he didn't have time to tell his wife. I don't know about other guys who are married, but I would be able to let my wife know if I was going somewhere no matter how short the notice was. Something is off with the whole family. The officers said the women wouldn't make eye contact with them and when they asked to speak to Missy they were told she went to spend time with her mother. There wasn't much they could do so they left. When they got to the precinct they had a couple of messages telling them it was a lie. Both messages said the same thing and were made by two different and unknown females. The way I see it is something stinks down at the Flowers farm."

Captain Morgan nodded to the watch commander who continued with the duties.

"O'Malley and Warren, you two go investigate a little further out at the farm. With these anonymous messages we need to take the disappearance seriously. There's been rumors of some funny business, possibly drug related, out at that place. Practice your investigative skills and find something." The watch commander finished assigning duties and the officers began to head out to patrol.

Mike and Jump headed out to their car and started to pull out but were stopped by the Captain waving them down.

"What's up Captain?" Mike rolled down the window to address him.

"Be careful going out there. We've had officers go to investigate this place before and they've not been greeted very fondly. Some swear they received verbal threats to stay away or else. I'm sure something is up with this missing guy but the family rallies around each other and shuts up when asked about one of their own. They are armed to the max and don't mind letting anyone see them carrying. They all have concealed weapon permits and some enter sharp shooting contests and I'm told they're pretty damn good. But something seems fishy about that place so just know I've got my eye on things concerning Candie's Flowers. Watch your backs." He gave a firm slap on the door sending them on their way.

"That was weird," Jump commented as they pulled out into traffic.

"Yeah, makes me wonder what else has happened out there. Maybe we can sort of sneak on the place and look around before we talk to anyone." Mike opened up his bag and started eating his muffin.

Jump agreed and they discussed how they would do this. Jump had already looked up the place on his phone and saw it was a sizable spot. He suggested they try arriving via some back roads and see what exactly is growing at Candie's Acres of Flowers.

Chapter 30
Candie

"Dammit, Earl! You said you'd handle everything and get the police off our backs." Candie was on the phone with her police contact. She paid Earl Thompson a hefty sum each month to keep the prying eyes of law enforcement off her property. Earl had called to give her a heads up about the two officers currently making their way to her place.

Earl was a twenty-year man and had been on the take the last five years. He always did his job by the books so no one would suspect him. However, with five kids in or nearing college and a wife who only worked a couple of days a week at the mall, money was always an issue. When he had been called out to the Flowers farm one time to investigate reports of marijuana, he met Candie and that day changed the course of his life. She offered him a tidy sum each month just for a phone call. It was too tempting to pass up. Earl took the bribe and never regretted it. He never told anyone either, not even his wife. He really believed only two can keep a secret when one of them is dead and he wasn't planning on being the dead one any time soon.

"I couldn't stop them. I can't just say 'hey don't bother with them 'cause it would raise flags. Just go about your usual business, let them nose around and they'll be on their way soon." Earl managed to get Candie to calm down. He ended the call and then got back to work at his legitimate job.

Candie slammed the phone and yelled for her boys to come see her. "Looks like we are gonna' have some police coming by to investigate more on Hank's disappearance. Be cooperative but don't let them roam around. That damn Missy! She better not ever show her face around here 'cause I'm liable to just blow it right off her head." Candie stormed away and her boys just stared after her.

"Well, let's get busy being normal." Tommy Flowers was the unspoken leader of the brothers. He gave each of the remaining men a task to do so they would appear like legitimate business owners when the police showed up. By doing this, the back of the property which was the part Uncle Sam didn't know about, was currently missing any of the Flowers men and that was the exact area where Jump found a dirt road giving them access to the property. He and Mike began to snoop around, unnoticed.

Jump was not his usual cheerful self today and Mike had noticed.

"What's up with you today?"

"Nothing. Just got things on my mind is all."

"Want to talk about it?" Mike was aware of the financial strain Jump was feeling with his kids hitting college age. He wanted them all to go to the best schools but that takes money which was something police officers were always short on.

"Nah. Need to focus on what we're doing. Don't want any surprises." Jump kept a lookout for anyone hoping to surprise the officers. The patrol car slowly made its way down the road. When Mike spotted a building hidden behind the trees he asked Jump about it.

"What do you think it is?"

"Looks like a shed of some sort. Guess we better check it out." Jump replied. He pulled the patrol car to a stop and the two got out. They both had their hands on their guns and were looking around for anything or anyone suspicious. Satisfied that no one was watching them they headed toward the building to investigate it.

"Damn, it stinks out here. I hope that's just dead skunk or something and not some rotting Flowers body inside."

Both men instinctively looked around the building for something possibly hidden.

"I think I found the source of the smell." Mike had made his way to the side of the building and found the dead Doberman near the bushes.

"All I see is the head and some ribs. Maybe a paw too. Shit, I could've gone my whole life and not seen that." Jump stated as he looked at the remains of the dog.

"Looks like nature has reclaimed this dog. Wonder why they just left it here to rot?"

Mike turned away and resumed his progress toward the porch first. Jump also followed, both men leaving the dog where it was. As they reached the front stoop they quietly stepped on it. Neither officer wanted a squeaky board announcing their presence.

"I've got a creepy feeling about this place." Mike said.

"Yeah, something ain't right here." Jump made his way to the window facing the porch and tried to peer in through the dirty panes. The filth on it was too great to see inside and there appeared to be a curtain of some sort blocking the view anyway. The two officers continued their investigation of the outside of the building. Both men unaware they were being investigated as well.

Silent Rage

Across the road and hidden behind some trees and brush Russell Thomas was observing the men make their way around the shed. Russell thought to himself that they needed to be more alert since he was able to watch them which, in Russell's mind, meant just about anyone could sneak up on the officers and cause them harm or worse. He decided he wanted to see just how close he could get without being noticed. It would be good soldier training for him. Russell moved very stealthily across the road, keeping himself low to the ground and hidden behind the undergrowth in the area and then the patrol car. He moved up to the porch and quietly walked to the side of the building so he would be out of the way of the windows and door. He could hear the two men moving around inside.

Mike and Jump had cleared the interior and felt safe that they were alone. Once they entered the building they knew they had found a meth lab so they cautiously checked out the entire place before they began looking around at the contents. In terms of a meth lab it was fairly well organized. It wasn't the usual burned out shell of an old mobile home that made the lethal concoction. This place was stocked full of all the ingredients needed to make pounds of methamphetamine. The cabinets held multiple boxes of products containing Ephedrine or Pseudoephedrine. This place could stock the whole town if a cold epidemic broke out and there were enough diet pills to make all the women look anorexic. There were multiple lab vials and beakers as well as huge pots along with their lids which were used for actually cooking the stuff. Oddly, there were multiple two liter bottles of soda as well.

Mike wondered about the soda. "Guess they get thirsty when they cook."

"Nah man, it's a new way to make it called 'shake and bake.'"

"How the hell do you know that? Mike asked.

"Unlike you, I actually read the reports that come out. This is the latest way to make the stuff fast and get it out on the streets."

"This is sick." Mike couldn't believe all he was seeing and just thinking about the number of people this crap would end up hurting was disturbing.

"Hey, Mike. Check this out." Jump was looking in some sort of hidden closet that contained a crate that was locked up.

"Wonder what's in there?" Mike was also examining the box and seeing if there was a way to open it. Both men tried to open the box but were unable to do so. They looked on all sides of the wooden chest but couldn't find any other way in.

"Should we bust it open? Could have a body in it?" Mike said.

"Don't smell like one is in there but ya' never know."

"Well let's find something to pry the lid open with. Wish we had a key."

"Wait, you hear something?" Jump quietly walked over to the window and peered outside.

Chapter 31
Libby

The next morning Libby locked her front door and headed to her car. The morning had just a hint of the cool air that signals the arrival of fall. It was the kind of day that made a person appreciate summer but eager for the coming cooler days. Even the air smelled crisp and clean. Libby started her car and headed to school. Her mind was still full of thoughts about Russell and she was beginning to formulate a plan and wanted to discuss it with Essie. She would have the opportunity to do just that since she was picking up Essie and driving her to school while her car was getting repaired. The insurance company didn't think the car was a total loss and agreed to repair it rather than replace the Volkswagen. She just hoped it was sanitized and smelled good.

Essie's apartment was in the heart of the city and happened to have a Starbucks right beside the entrance to her building. Essie was standing on the sidewalk waiting for Libby and holding two steaming cups of the addictive brew. Libby pulled to the curb and reached across the seat to open the door for Essie. "Here ya' go. One Grande extra hot skinny two pump mocha for you and one caramel macchiato fully loaded for me." Essie handed the cup to Libby who took a deep breath and sighed.

"Ahhhh, and people wonder why I like you." Libby laughed and took a sip of her coffee.

"I have good news. Well sort of anyway."

"What?" asked Libby.

"My car will be ready this afternoon. If you could drive me to Tommy's Garage I would greatly appreciate it."

"Of course I will. I hope the car is as good as new and there are no lingering side effects or odors!"

"You and me both!" Essie said as she took a big sip of her coffee.

The two teachers chatted about their plans for the weekend and other topics as they drove to school for their morning duties. As they went their separate ways Libby asked Essie to come to her room at lunch because she had something she wanted to run by her.

The morning passed uneventfully and Libby was able to get through her lessons without any hiccups. That was always a good thing when it came to teaching middle schoolers. It seems there was inevitably some crisis in one of the students' lives, usually revolving around boys or sports. Her female students often whispered to Libby "That's the boy I like" and her male students were busy acting as if they were the next pro athlete walking around campus. The drama in their young lives always made Libby smile. If only life was always that carefree. A sudden loud roar coming from the hallway caused Libby to run out to see what was going on. In the middle of the hall it appeared that two boys were fighting. Libby quickly saw they both happened to be students of hers so she ran and jumped in the middle of them and yelled for one boy to stand at the wall while she held the other by his shoulders and tried to calm him down.

"What's going on?" Libby asked the young boy she was talking to and could feel his heart beat racing even through her hands on his shoulders.

Silent Rage

"Russell called me a retard and I'm sick of everyone picking on me just 'cause I go to resource for reading." Libby couldn't help but feel sorry for the boy. She knew he had difficulty reading because he was dyslexic and that was something the other kids didn't know. They routinely called him names and she couldn't fault the boy for finally blowing up and hitting someone. "Tell me what happened."

The young man, Eric, explained that all the kids were teasing him during gym. Russell walked past him in the hall and whispered "retard" and Eric said he just lost it and turned around and slugged Russell on the back. Libby had to admire the courage of Eric since Russell was known to be a scrappy kid himself. Libby instructed the youth to sit in her classroom while she talked with Russell. Just then a school assistant principal came hurrying down the hall. It would appear word finally reached the office that a fight had occurred.

"I'll handle this Miss Teach," said the female administrator who was known to be extra tough on fighters.

"It's OK, I've got it under control and there was really no altercation merely an exchange of words." Libby was trying to keep her students from getting suspended since the "zero tolerance" rules applied to fighting.

"It doesn't matter what was said if there was any exchanging of fists then they will both be suspended and possibly expelled. We will look at the video from the hall cameras and make a decision." Libby could tell this woman was not going to let it slide.

"All right, I will escort the other student to you as soon as he gets his books." Libby wanted a moment to hear Russell's side and thought this was probably her only chance. The administrator nodded her agreement and then looked at Eric and told him to collect his belongings and follow her. Eric picked up his book bag and slowly headed down the hall toward the offices at the front of the school. The administrator's shoes could be heard making a staccato click all the way down the hall and around the corner. Libby sighed and then turned and headed in the opposite direction down the hall toward her room to retrieve Russell and hopefully have a few positive words with him before he got suspended

Russell was waiting in her classroom with his head resting on his fists on top of the desk. He was visibly upset. Libby asked him to tell her what prompted the fight and he slowly told her the story of the bullying he went through every day at school. Today during gym, the other boys were picking on Eric and calling him names and Russell, who simply wanted to fit in, also said some insulting words to Eric. When the other boys noticed Russell joining in, they quickly invited him to sit at their lunch table if he could get Eric in trouble and sent to the office. This actually encouraged Russell because he usually sat by himself at lunch. If he could get Eric in trouble he might possibly have some new friends. Libby's heart broke for Russell who only wanted to belong. She understood his behavior and almost sided with him although she wished the fight hadn't occurred. The reality was, however, the boys who insisted Russell could sit at their table would probably not have let him and were just adding another victim to their bullying.

Libby walked with Russell to the office and said she would do what she could to keep him in school but she wasn't hopeful. Once in the assistant principal's office the administrator instructed Libby to return to class. Libby tried to explain the circumstances surrounding the fight but the stern supervisor would hear nothing of it and simply said "zero tolerance, end of story." Libby resumed her afternoon classes but kept the boys and Russell in particular, in the back of her mind. The rest of the day passed without incident. Just after the afternoon dismissal bell, Essie showed up at Libby's door. "You ready to go get my car?"

"Sure am, just let me pack up my computer. How was your day?"

"Not as exciting as yours I hear."

"So you heard about the fight?" Libby turned off the lights in her room and left her door open in preparation for the afternoon cleaning crew to sweep her floor. Libby and Essie made their way to the parking lot.

"I couldn't help but hear about it since that was all my students wanted to talk about. Eric is a quiet kid and never bothers anybody so for him to actually hit someone was quite the topic for everyone. I believe they actually have a new admiration for Eric so maybe when he returns from his suspension he will have an easier time of things."

"I hope so. Did you know that Russell was basically bullied into punching Eric?" Libby asked. She looked both ways and then merged her car into the school traffic on the street.

"How so?"

"Russell told me the boys in gym class were picking on Eric. Russell felt sorry for the guy but for some reason when he walked past Russell, Eric called him a retard. Russell said he is sick of everyone calling him names so he

152

just reacted and hit Eric. One thing led to another and now Russell is suspended."

"That poor kid doesn't ever seem to get a break."

"No he doesn't and it's not the first time he's been bullied," Libby said.

Libby mentioned how he really had no friends and at his age lunchtime was a big stress factor for kids who didn't have a group to sit with. Middle schoolers could be brutal when it came to making someone an outcast. Soon, however, their talk turned to other things including the budding romance between Essie and Stan. They giggled and talked about the future the two might have someday. As they pulled into the car repair shop's lot they saw Essie's bright yellow car parked out front. They eagerly got out to go see the repairs.

"Well, it definitely smells better!" this from Essie as she stuck her head into her shiny and freshly washed car. Libby also put her head in the car to get a whiff of the repairs.

"We replaced all the upholstery and even put in new seats in the front for you. We just couldn't get out all the stains on the original seats." Tommy of Tommy's Garage wiped his hands on the perpetual grease rag he had in his back pocket. He could wipe all day and he still wouldn't remove the years of grime and grease that coated his hands. He was one of the best mechanics in town and was known for his honesty and hard work ethic making it easy to overlook his stained hands.

"The car is beautiful and looks so much better than I thought it might. I really can't tell it was ever vandalized." Essie was beaming at her car. Tommy settled up her portion of the remaining bill and gave her the keys. "I can't wait to take her for a spin! You even got her eyelashes put back on!" Tommy grinned and said he and his team felt kind of silly putting them on but they knew Essie would want them. Obviously Essie had worked her charm on the burly men at the shop and they would do just about anything to make her happy. Essie waved goodbye to everybody and took off in her newly repaired VW Bug. Libby couldn't help but smile at the goofy grins on the faces of all the mechanics as they waved bye to Essie. That girl just had a way with men.

Libby found herself with a free evening since Mike was on patrol. She was worried about how things might be at home for Russell so she decided to drive out to his house and check on him under the guise of bringing him his assignments.

As she pulled onto the street where Russell lived, Libby couldn't help but shudder at the eerie quiet that ensconced the area. It wasn't that late but it looked like everyone had their lights off in their homes. She parked her car as close to Russell's trailer as she could get. Grabbing her tote bag which was full of assignments for Russell, Libby closed her car door and used her remote to lock it. She even locked it twice just to be safe. The reassuring beep gave her a false sense of security. Maybe it was just normal to be this dark around here. Libby made her way to the door and knocked on it. Dreading having to explain her reason for visiting to the disgusting human being who shared the home with Russell and his mom, Libby was pleasantly surprised to see Russell open the door.

"Hey, Miss Teach. What are you doing here?"

"Good evening Russell. I just wanted to check on you and make sure you're ok and also to bring you some assignments so that you don't fall behind in school." Libby held out the tote bag of work for Russell to take. When he reached for the bag his shirt sleeves rode up his skinny arm a bit and Libby noticed a series of bright red marks encircling his upper arm. Clearly someone had grabbed Russell and the mark would leave a bruise before long. "Russell, what happened? That looks painful."

Russell quickly tugged the sleeve of his shirt down and covered the sign of abuse and shrugged his shoulders. "It's nothing. I don't want to talk about it. Thanks for the work." Russell attempted to close the door but Libby stuck her foot in the opening to keep it from closing.

"Russell, you don't have to put up with this kind of treatment. I can help you if you want it." Libby felt some kind of unexplained bond with the troubled youth. In the dark recesses of her mind she remembered how Uncle Roger made her feel when he abused her years ago. Those kinds of scars are hard to erase. Libby supposed that was why she felt some kind of affection for Russell, a shared history of abuse although his appeared to be much worse.

"Miss Teach you really just need to go. I'm fine and my momma will be home soon." That was a lie because Russell didn't know when his mother would come in from evening at work. He knew she had been having to work longer hours. He guessed it was because her broken arm slowed her down.

Libby didn't have much choice other than to trust what Russell was telling her and leave him alone. She said goodnight and he closed the door and turned off the lights casting Libby in even more darkness since her eyes had grown accustomed to the light. She reached for a handrail but found none so she had to gingerly place her foot in front of her feeling for the step down to the dirt in front of the stoop. Stepping down tentatively until she felt solid ground Libby was relieved to be able to quickly head to her car.

As she took another step she didn't see the pothole and stepped right into a deep pit. She fell forward and tried to catch herself with her hands. Managing to keep from falling flat on her face, Libby pulled herself out of the hole and got to her feet. Her hands were scraped and cut and her knee hurt as did her ankle. Standing up and brushing herself off she noticed the tear in her pants. "Dammit! These were my favorite pants," Libby said out loud to herself and simultaneously wondered why she even cared about her pants. Stomping her feet and grunting in frustration Libby limped to her car. The good news was her eyes had become adjusted to the dark so maybe she wouldn't fall again. Her ankle felt like it was only slightly twisted.

Pulling the car keys out of her pocket Libby pressed the button to unlock the Jetta. As she did the headlights flashed at her and caused her to see something out of place about her car. It appeared to be uneven for some reason. Libby examined the car and noticed the driver's side tire looked flat. "Oh no!" exclaimed Libby and she bent to look at the tire. As she bent down she placed her hand against the car and she noticed the long mark left by a mean vandal along the side of her car. Libby screamed in frustration and reached in her pocket for her phone. At that precise moment a dark figure rushed at Libby and hit her over the head with a baseball bat. She immediately fell to the ground unconscious. Her phone dropped from her hands and bumped over to a nearby bush where it settled just out of sight. Her attacker picked her up and threw her over his shoulders and hurried away into the darkness of the surrounding woods.

Inside the Thomas' trailer Russell peered out of the window and saw his teacher get carried away. Seeing his teacher get carried away was the second thing Russell had observed getting carted off that day.

Earlier Russell had been exploring in the woods and went to check on the progress of the two dead bodies he had discovered a few days ago. The bodies were rapidly decomposing since they were out in the elements. Animal activity was obvious from the teeth marks on the hands of the dead men plus some of their fingers were missing. Russell figured a coyote or something made a meal out of them. Another thing that fascinated Russell was that the skin of the two victims had darkened and some bones were already visible. The scalp of one of the dead men was already sliding off his head. Russell wanted to keep it because he thought it would be a cool thing to have, sort of like an old Indian war trophy a warrior kept from a scalping victim.

He set up some rocks around the bodies to make the scene look like a burial site. This served a twofold purpose for him. One it gave him a place to sit when he watched the activity going on around the dead bodies and two, it made the place look like a sacrificial area where warriors brought their captives. Russell worked quietly and began to notice the forest seemed quieter than usual. It made him go on alert, this is good practice for sneaking up on enemy forces he thought to himself.

He sat quietly on a rock near the bodies and made very little noise and listened to his surroundings. Russell thought he heard some voices so he got up and made his way to some nearby trees where he could hide and take a look around him. He realized he was near a building that Russell knew was used for making drugs. He had read enough crime to know he was probably looking at a meth lab plus he had overheard a couple of men talking about a meth lab and the men had guns. He knew he did not want to get caught by those guys. No telling what they'd do to him.

From his hiding place, Russell saw a police car parked in front of the old building. He crept closer and made his way to a side window he knew was partially opened. He climbed up on some rocks, which he had moved there on another clandestine visit, and peaked in the windows. He saw two police officers looking through the closets and cabinets inside. He quietly watched them as they searched the place.

He could tell the men found something because one of them said he wished he had a key for some chest they were looking at. Russell tried to pull himself up on the edge of the window frame to see what they were doing but his foot slid and banged against the building making a soft thud. He crouched down behind the bush and hoped it gave him adequate cover. He couldn't see the face that appeared in the window directly above him. Neither could they see the boy hiding in the bushes directly below.

Chapter 32
Mike

Mike was looking inside of a cabinet when he heard a noise. "Did you hear that?"

"Yeah, I'll check it out." Jump walked over to peer out of the window but backed away from it when he didn't see anything. "I don't see anybody. Probably a rat I heard. This place must attract all kinds of vermin. Furry and human alike. Well, maybe the assholes left a key hidden somewhere."

Mike laughed at that and said; "Meth heads aren't known for being the smartest dicks out there so maybe they left the key on the top of the door frame."

"We should be so lucky," Jump said as he searched up to search the top of the frame, just in case. Not finding anything there he slid his hands down the sides of the door.

"Well, nothing on the top of the door but look what I found!" Jump held a key up for Mike to see.

"Where was that?' Mike asked.

"Hanging on the side of the frame. Let's see if it fits." Jump inserted the key and opened the trunk. "Damn."

Both men stood in astonished silence as they gazed at the contents of the chest.

"Shit! Is that real?" Mike asked as he looked over Jump's shoulder.

"Looks real to me." Jump reached into the chest and picked up a wad of hundred dollar bills. All nice and clean and bunched together as if it just rolled off the printing press.

"How much you think that is?" Jump asked.

"I don't know. Maybe a half a million dollars," Mike commented.

"Who says crime doesn't pay. Sure could use that myself," Mike said.

"Yeah, me too. Got that college expense coming up and this would make my life so much easier. Hah! What say we just take it and don't tell anyone?" Jump joked.

"If only it were so easy. It really sucks that the scumbags that make all this shit also get so much cash, and tax free I might add," Mike said.

"Sure ya' don't wanna' just keep it for ourselves? Seems the lowlifes who buy this crap owe us a bonus and I'm looking at it." Jump was warming up to the idea of simply keeping the money.

"We can't do that! You're not serious, are you?" Mike was shocked that Jump would even think about it but he did have to admit he could use it too. It would go a long way in making the house he was buying a home for him and Libby.

"Who would know if we did?" Jump said.

The two cops continued their discussion about how they could actually take the money and get away with it. Neither man really thought the other would do it but it was fun to think about. However, the more they talked the more they realized they could take the money and get away with it. Who would know?

"Ok, so say we take it. Sarge sent us out here and knows we're here. If someone says their money is gone we'll be the first ones they question," Mike said.

"Well, think Mike. We're at an illegal meth lab. The guys that run this baby are looking at a long time in prison. Think they're going rat on us? They can't admit this place

160

exists. So we put the chest in the trunk of our car and call it in. No one is going to look in a cop car for a missing box of cash." Jump was justifying their taking the money.

They kept going over all the possible scenarios and finally decided they could actually get away with it. Both men slid the chest out of the closet and carried it to the patrol car. After placing it in the trunk of the car, they shut the lid and looked at each other. They both realized they had crossed a line they neither of them ever thought they would. It was sobering.

Mike stood and stretched his back. "Last chance to back out."

Both men were quiet as they thought about what they were about to do.

"Let's call it in," Jump said.

Mike made the call and the two went back in to make sure they didn't leave any obvious signs of a recently missing box from the closet.

Russell had remained hidden during the entire exchange between the officers. He was scared. He knew what just happened was bad and he knew the men who made the drugs in the lab would be real mad. He just wanted to get away and pretend he never saw a thing. He quietly backed away from the window and made his way into the darkening woods. Once concealed by the trees he began to run home. He didn't want to examine the dead bodies anymore, he just wanted to get out of there.

Chapter 33
Libby

Libby awoke with a massive headache and an awful taste in her mouth. She tried to rub her head but found she couldn't move her hands. They were tied behind her back to the chair she was sitting in and her mouth was gagged with a foul smelling rag. She hoped it was somehow clean but didn't feel optimistic. As she became more alert she began to take in her surroundings. She appeared to be in some kind of storage shed. It looked like it was only one room and she could see that there was a variety of old tools either hanging from the ceiling or resting against the walls. There was also an old table which held some rotted buckets and plastic pots. *This must have been someone's potting shed at some point in history,* Libby thought.

Libby groaned and weakly called out a hello but received no response. Not even the chirping of insects greeted her back. She tried to pull her hands free but couldn't get them to budge. There was a case of bottled water on the floor near her but she couldn't even try to get one with her hands tied. Seeing the water made he realize she was incredibly thirsty and it was pure torture to have the water so close and yet so far. Why had someone kidnapped her? She couldn't begin to think of what value she would be to a criminal. She didn't know whether or not the water bottles meant someone wanted her alive and was coming back to eventually let her go and if so was that a good thing or a bad thing? Trying not to panic Libby decided to take stock of her situation and determine how to get herself out of it.

Silent Rage

The shed had one window that was covered in dirt and grime but was slightly open to allow a breeze to enter the building. She was thankful for that consideration if her abductor had opened it. She also noted it was light outside so it must be sometime Saturday. She didn't think she had been out too long and the brightness just didn't seem like an afternoon sun. So she has been missing for maybe 12 hours. No one would notice just yet. Mike was working late shifts all weekend and would be asleep now. Besides he wouldn't call her, most likely he only sent her a text. That means he won't notice she wasn't replying until later in the day and he may just think she is busy and will talk to him Monday. That was not an unusual scenario on weekends when he worked.

Libby squirmed in frustration. Then she realized nature was calling. There were plenty of buckets to use if she could get to one. She tried to pull her hands free one more time but with no luck. She did, however, realize her feet were not bound. It took a couple of tries but she was able to stand and even maneuver around, although awkwardly since she had a chair attached to her back. She couldn't figure out how to get her pants down in order to relieve herself and finally decided it was pointless to try to save the pants since they were ruined anyway. Using her feet to move a bucket between her legs she tried to squat and relieve herself.

"Oh for Pete's sake!" Libby screamed in frustration when she realized that wetting her pants didn't require the use of a bucket since the liquid simply spread out in her pants and ran down her legs. "Yuck, yuck, yuck! Someone will pay!" Libby was just about reduced to tears but wouldn't let herself give in and make her kidnapper happy.

Besides crying wouldn't accomplish anything except make her feel like a helpless female. Taking a deep breath, she next tackled the problem of getting water.

Libby sort of hopped-walked over to the case of water bottles and stared at them while she tried to come up with a way to get one. She noticed they had expired over three months ago. Well, at this point what did it matter anyway, if she actually managed to drink the out of date water. It was better than nothing. After studying her situation she was able to come up with a way she hoped would allow her to get a water bottle opened and then actually drink it. She used one of the legs of the chair to poke a hole in the plastic surrounding the bottles. Then, moving her body she was able to get the chair leg to rip the opening wider so she could free one of the bottles. Without the use of her hands this part would be a challenge. Using her foot, she managed to get the toe of her shoe in and work on wiggling the bottle out until it finally fell over. It was free enough that Libby could pick up the bottle if she could just get her hands on it. Standing up straight, because her back was killing her, Libby once again studied her situation. Catching her breath and trying to stretch out her aching back muscles, Libby determined she needed to sit down in order to get the water bottle.

Easing the chair back as slowly as she could, Libby tried to sit down. She miscalculated and ended up falling completely on her back with her legs in the air. Now she was ready to cry because it really hurt her hands when she fell on them. Looking around for the bottle of water Libby saw that she had fallen right beside it and by rolling on to her side her hands could grasp the water bottle and open it. Once it was open Libby placed it standing upright and then started the slow process of sliding herself around to where her mouth could reach the top of the bottle. She prayed she didn't knock the bottle over before she drank its contents.

Feeling like an overgrown worm, Libby slowly rolled and slid and got herself in position to put her lips on the bottle opening. Using her teeth as a vice she was able to turn the bottle up and get the liquid to slide down her parched throat as well as her face and neck. She drank the entire bottle mostly because she was so thirsty but also because she didn't want to go through getting another bottle for a while. "At least I don't have to get in a workout in today," Libby said to no one.

Now that she had finished the water she needed to get herself back to an upright position, preferably standing. She thought if she could somehow get to her knees she would be able to push herself back up. As she tried to maneuver herself to an upright position she heard someone coming which caused her to freeze in terror.

Chapter 34
Flowers Farm

"What do you mean it's gone?" Candie yelled at her son, Butch. He was the one who had to give the news about the missing money to his mother. It was a task he dreaded. Candie had a violent temper and was not above taking a fist or any object close by to her grown sons. They were currently in the office of the legitimate part of the business and Candie was working on ordering bulbs for the flower farm. She quickly rose up from the leather chair she was sitting in causing it to teeter back and forth on its wheeled legs and slide backward. It was as if even the chair wanted to get away from Candie's temper.

"This better be some kind of sick joke. There was over a half a million dollars in that chest." Candie stepped closer to Butch and poked him in the chest with her long boney finger emphasizing each word she said. Butch tried to back away but he was already at the wall and Candie wasn't going in the other direction.

"I know, Mama, I helped count it." Butch had his hands up trying to grab Candie's wrists and keep her from slapping him.

"Well, what the hell happened?" Candie turned away from Butch and began pacing the small office.

"The cops came out and found the shed. They've got it taped off but me and Timmy went in after they left to check things out. They confiscated all the shit we had stashed for the meth."

"That's the least of my worries. That can be replaced but a half a million damn dollars can't!" Candie was getting madder by the minute. Butch just wanted to get out of there. "So the chest was gone and you checked all over the place? Any chance you moved it and forgot or maybe Hank or John did and didn't tell ya'?"

"No mama. We knew exactly where that chest was and how much money was in it. It was hidden in the back of a closet and ya' had to know it was there to even see it."

"Do you think those two idiots Lucky Sam sent over found it?" asked Candie.

"That's what Hank thinks. They shot up the place and must've gotten Hank or John to give 'em the money maybe in exchange for their lives."

"Well, hell, we ain't even seen them. I hope they didn't take the money and run."

"No chance of that. They had plans and were the ones who put the chest in the closet anyway. I don't think they would've cheated us. I think those assholes Lucky Sam sent over somehow found it and stole it." Butch would say anything to get his mom to calm down. Truth was, he didn't know who took the money and Hank could very well have decided to pack up and leave. Maybe he told Missy to meet him somewhere.

"That bitch Missy. This is all her fault for calling the damn police. We don't have the lab and now we don't even have the money. How the hell are we supposed to get that cash back?" Candie was working herself into a state and Butch figured he'd better get out of there before all hell broke loose.

"Let me and Timmy take care of this. We'll go talk to Lucky Sam and see what's up."

"I guess that's all we can do right now. It's not like I can report this theft to the police." Candie picked up her coffee cup and threw it across the room barely missing

Butch's head. "Damn. I'm so mad I could spit nails. You better find that money or you and your brother and any other employee I got are gonna be working for free! Permanently!"

"Don't worry about it. We'll get the cash back. Timmy's already working on building another lab and we can start getting the stuff to cook some meth. It'll be ok." Butch left the room quickly and went to find Timmy so they could pay a visit to Lucky Sam's place of business just like those two goons had done to theirs.

Chapter 35
Libby

The bulky form of Wayne appeared in the doorway to the shed where Libby was being held captive.

"'Bout time you woke up. I ain't into sex with comatose females." Wayne snarled with a wicked leer. Libby was too afraid to move, let alone breathe. Her arms were beginning to seriously hurt and she ached all over. She was on the verge of tears but refused to let this lowlife see her cry.

Wayne walked over and yanked the chair to an upright position. As he did so he pulled her shirt up and gave each of her breasts a squeeze. Libby tightly closed her eyes.

"Stop it!" She yelled.

"You ain't in no position to tell me what to do. The way I see it I am in total control over you." Wayne gave his crotch a yank and continued, "I am going to teach you, little Miss Teacher, just who is in charge of this here classroom."

Libby was now beyond caring if he saw her cry. Tears were streaming down her cheeks but she was still equal parts afraid and mad. She vowed to make sure this man spent the rest of his life behind bars.

"You may be able to do things to my body that are beyond my control and believe me, the only way you could ever get a girl to do anything to you is by tying her up." Libby never could control her mouth and her taunt enraged Wayne and he promptly slapped her several times.

Libby gasped and spat back at him, "You are nothing but a fat, butt-ugly, loser. I pity Loretta and Russell having to live with you."

"Live is the key word. They get to live but when I'm through with you there won't be nothing left worth living for." Wayne began to unbuckle his belt and took a step toward Libby.

Outside of the shed Russell was silently watching the events unfolding inside. He was torn as to whether or not to interrupt and help his beloved teacher or just leave and come back later and get her out of there. He knew if he intervened with Wayne there would be a terrible price to pay. Wayne would be incredibly mad at Russell and would make him do even more than just the nasty like he usually did when he was in a bad mood. Russell shuddered at the memory of things Wayne had made him do. He never wanted to do some of them ever again so he determined he would leave and help Libby later. Russell was so tired of Wayne and so he figured his teacher could handle it and he would just return once Wayne left.

Wayne ripped Libby's blouse off to fully expose her to his malicious gaze. He fondled her breasts through her red bra and then he laughed when he discovered the garment hooked in the front.

"I love front snaps. Makes me able to get at the goodies much easier." Wayne unhooked the bra and then pushed Libby backward causing her chair to topple over again making her hit her head. "Now it's time to give you some one-on-one tutorials in the fine of art of pleasing a man." Wayne then proceeded to pull Libby's pants down exposing her red thong. All Wayne could think to say was, "Damn!"

Russell watched Wayne as he continued to assault Libby and vowed he would make sure Wayne paid for what he did. Just then he heard some voices coming through the trees.

"Hey, look what we got here!" One of the guys Russell knew was selling drugs grabbed him before he could make a quick getaway. "What are you doing out here, kid?"

Russell knew this guy was the leader and the two hiding behind him did whatever he said. Russell didn't want them to take him to Wayne. The penalty for spying would be unimaginable. Just then a scream pierced the night and the sudden noise caused the drug dealer to look away giving Russell the chance to break free and run into to the woods.

Libby trembled at the sight of the three men entering the shed. Her mind automatically created scenes she did not want to be a part of with these creatures. They now stood leering at her nakedness.

"Hey man, you didn't say you was going to have some fun with the lady," said the newcomer in the front. Libby recognized him as one of the guys who threatened her about coming back. She was terrified at what might happen now. "But as much as I want to stay and have some fun we've got a little problem up near the house."

Wayne was now standing over Libby and zipping up his pants. He was irritated his session with the teacher had been interrupted. Someone would have to pay later, he thought to himself, and it was a good thing Loretta was out and he could make that loser kid of hers take care of his frustration.

"What are you talking about? What kind of situation?" Wayne asked.

"Police are here."

"Shit. You idiots can't take care of anything without my telling you how to do it." This was said as the four men left the shed and Libby lying on the floor barely clothed. They didn't even glance back at her, not that she wanted them to. As their voices faded away Libby then gave in to her tears and cried.

Chapter 36
Flowers Farm

Butch and Timmy Flowers had their .38's stuffed in the back of their jeans as they headed out to one of the few remaining farm trucks. Butch got in on the driver's side and Timmy rode shotgun. It was a Flowers family rule the oldest male always drove. While Butch hated that his brothers weren't around to deal with this recent mess, he was sort of proud he got to be the alpha male right then.

"Guess we need to ride over to Sassy A and have a few words with those jackasses," Timmy said. He was the youngest of the brothers. Timmy was somewhat of a hothead and always ready to throw a punch before taking the time to solve a problem with words. Not always a good trait to have but it often served the brothers well when dealing with the scum who bought their illegal product.

"I think we need to have some sort of plan for dealing with them. If we just waltz in there they may shoot us," Butch said. Butch could only be described as a lover not a fighter. Even now he was looking at his reflection in the rearview mirror and rubbing his hand over his perfectly groomed five o'clock shadow. As the best looking of the brothers he always had his fair share of women around and he did not like to do anything that might permanently mess up his good looks. Hence, his aversion to fighting.

"I think we should just go in quick with guns blazing and whoever is in the way too bad for them. Then we leave and tell them not to mess with the Flowers Farm or next time there'd be dead bodies from the bullets," Timmy replied.

"No, idiot. This isn't some damn western. They already warned us not to do anything so I think we've got to be sneaky. Maybe wait in the parking lot for one of them twins to come out and then fire a warning shot at him. Then leave real quick-like and make them all nervous about what might be next."

Timmy gave that idea some thought and decided it sounded okay to him even though he was disappointed he wouldn't be able to punch someone. Butch cranked up the truck giving the gas pedal an extra-long push just to make the engine roar loudly. The two brothers discussed their game plan of just how they would accomplish their surprise attack as they drove over to the bar.

Meanwhile, in the bar, the two Berts were bragging to Lucky Sam about the fate of the Flowers men and still reliving their adventures from a few nights ago. They tended to embellish their exploits and Sam was certainly aware of it. He let the two ramble on before finally asking them about the product.

"So you took care of them selling anymore product on my premises? And I'm now the owner of their so called establishment, correct?" Lucky Sam asked.

"Yeah, boss. We made sure the rest of them knew you would be calling the shots now and they won't be stopping it or they'll end up dead like their relatives." Dalbert snickered at the comment. The two brothers were standing in front of Lucky Sam's big mahogany desk in his office. The desk had come from the office of an investment banker who ended up having an expensive addiction and owed quite a lot to Sam. In order to pay off his debt he agreed to part with his custom made and beloved office desk. It was a unique desk that cost him over a hundred thousand dollars and Sam had once admired the piece when he paid a visit to the banker. When the banker couldn't pay-up Sam was happy to work out a deal. The banker, though upset at losing his prized possession, was relieved he would not be facing the two Berts some night in a back alley. Sam was tapping his fingers on the now infamous desk while he listened to his hired enforcers.

"Okay. So get on out front and keep an eye out for anything else. It's been quiet for a few days now and I sense trouble is coming. Those dumbasses may try to get some payback. It's what I'd do if someone shot up my place of business. Got to expect them to do something stupid." Sam was a savvy businessman and was rarely if ever caught unprepared for some blowback from a bad deal. He always thought of what he would do to retaliate and then get ready for it. This plan worked for him so far and he saw no reason it wouldn't continue to serve him well when dealing with the new meth-heads who'd be coming to him for their fix.

"Go grab yourselves a beer," Sam said as he dismissed the brothers.

The two Berts left the office and headed to the front door. They took up their positions and signaled for the bartender to bring them a beer. Lucky Sam didn't allow his employees to drink on the job unless one of his girls was entertaining a customer in the back. He occasionally let the Berts have a beer when they'd completed an especially strenuous assignment. Tonight was one of those times the guys were allowed to enjoy a beer on company time.

Chapter 37
Butch and Timmy

The two Flowers brothers were sitting in their truck in the parking lot of Sassy A. They were waiting for one or even both of the Berts to leave the bar and head to their truck. They knew which car belonged to the brothers because they stole one of the Flowers Farm trucks and the name was right there on the front door of the pick-up.

"Damn that makes me mad they just took one of our trucks," Butch said.

"Yeah, I feel like walking right up to them and shoving my gun in their ugly mugs and just shooting 'em," Timmy replied. He was still mad and itching for a fight.

"Well, then you'd just be a dead asshole 'cause the one you didn't shoot first would just shoot you," said Butch.

Timmy just grunted because he didn't want to admit his brother had a point. Just then the door to the club opened and both Berts came out carrying bottles of beers. One of them said something funny and they both laughed and took long swallows of their drinks. They leaned against the building and appeared to be taking a break from their duties inside.

"This seems like as good time as any to let them know not to mess with us," Butch said to Timmy.

"So you just gonna ride by and we both just shoot or what?" Timmy asked.

"Yeah, we can both just aim above them and scare them. They'll know it's us 'cause of the truck."

"OK, let's do it."

Silent Rage

What happened next would change the fate of both the Flowers family and Sassy A forever. The truck rode by and Timmy and Butch aimed their guns at what they thought was above the heads of the Berts. They fired and one of the big twins ducked down but the other stayed standing and as he turned to look at the place where the shots came from, another one rang out and exploded his head leaving brain matter all over the side of Sassy A. The remaining brother howled in anger and grief when he saw his brother. It was as if that inexplicable twin connection was making him feel the pain from his brother's head. The truck screeched out of the parking lot but not before a patron with plans to enter the club made a mental note of the truck and license plate as he called 911 for the fallen Bert.

Chapter 38
Mike

Several hours later and still at the scene of the shooting, the detectives who drew the case determined that the murder of Albert Moore was drug-related and probably over a turf war. When Mike and John arrived on the scene, they overheard a couple of officers talking about the Flowers Farm and the missing men and how evidently a meth lab was located in a hidden spot on the farm. The two officers looked at each other, grinned, and got back to doing their job. They felt a lot like Dalbert must feel about then—they had dodged a bullet. Jump winked at Mike.

"Not another word. Ever."

Mike silently nodded to his partner. The two men put a long night and were finally able to call it a day and head home to get some much needed rest.

The buzzing of the world's largest fly was annoying the crap out of Mike. He swatted at the thing but it kept right on pestering him. That was when he realized it was his phone on the nightstand by his bed. It was vibrating an alert that he had an incoming call. *What the heck?* Mike thought. Everyone knew he just finished his shift and needed to get some sleep before his next rotation later that day. Looking to see who had the nerve to call him, he noticed it was Jump.

"What the hell you want, Jump?" Mike yelled into the phone.

"Hey man, I'm outside your place and I need you to come open the door. I've got some bad news." Mike quickly got out of bed and pulled on some clothes. He couldn't imagine what the bad news was. His family was

OK as far as he knew and Libby was safe at her apartment. Maybe this was about the money. He opened the door and Jump came in.

"What's up?" Mike asked.

"A car was found in the pond just past Spalding Avenue." Jump began.

"So. You woke me up for a car that probably belongs to some junkie?" Mike said.

"Let me finish. It's a red Jetta and the plates came back to Libby."

Mike immediately went pale and began to get weak in the knees. Jump quickly grabbed him and eased him onto the sofa nearby. "Is Libby…" he couldn't get the words out.

"No one was in the car. Divers are working the scene but so far there's been no sign of a body."

"Why would her car be over there? What was she doing?" Mike couldn't come up with a reason for her to be in the dangerous neighborhood.

Jump supplied the possible answer. "Didn't you tell me she has a student who lives on that street?"

"Oh no. Yeah, she does and for some reason she's made him her pet project. She thinks she can save him from a life of crime or something." Mike realized her altruistic efforts may have cost her more than either of them could have imagine. Tears began to form in his eyes. "I've got to get over there."

"I know man. I figured you would want to be there but I am driving you. So let's go."

Mike quickly grabbed his gun and shoes and ran out of the house.

Chapter 39
Libby

Libby held her breath as a shadow passed by the window. She was afraid it was her abductor and yet at the same time she was hoping it was him coming back to release her. She stared at the door and held her breath in fear and anticipation. She saw the door knob turn quietly, as if the person was trying to sneak in. Then a silhouette appeared in the doorway. She couldn't tell who it was because there was hardly any light filtering in behind him. Libby briefly wondered if it was night and just how long has she been tied up. She was squinting at the intruder and trying to decide whether or not to be scared. That was when she noticed the tire iron in his hand and felt terror creep into her soul. As he stepped into the room Libby saw it was Wayne and he looked like pure evil at that moment.

"What do you want and why did you kidnap me?" Libby shuddered as she asked her tormentor.

"Shut up! I'll ask the questions." Wayne raised the weapon as if he was about to hit Libby over the head with it but instead brought it down right beside her head causing her hair to blow back.

Libby flinched in anticipation of the pain and said a silent prayer she would somehow get out of this and make this creature pay.

"Now you tell me why you keep snooping around here or I'll split your head open and your cop lover will never see you again." Wayne stepped closer to Libby, righted her chair, and grabbed her hair making her look up at him.

Silent Rage

Libby couldn't stand being made to feel so helpless nor could she keep herself from fighting back even if it was currently with just her words.

"So Wayne, is this the only way you can get a girl? Tie her up and force her to cower to you? You're nothing but a loser and a pedophile. I'll make sure my boyfriend knows all about you."

"I know you're just trying to rile me and believe me, you'll soon know just how I like my women." Wayne grabbed his crotch and gave it a shake in Libby's face. She involuntarily recoiled. Wayne simply laughed and shoved his groin in her face. "Don't worry, we'll get to that in a minute but first tell me what your cop lover knows about my side business."

"What are you talking about? Mike doesn't talk to me about his work. I'm here for the sake of checking on Russell and I will be alerting the authorities about his situation. You better untie me and let me go and maybe someone will cut a deal with you." Libby had no idea what she was talking about, she merely knew it sounded good and like something that would be said on a detective show. She hoped she sounded convincing.

"Now I do like a feisty woman but I'm serious. Tell me what Mike knows or I'll make sure your pretty face never looks the same again."

"I do not know what you want to know. I am a teacher and I am just trying to help Russell. If you're in trouble talk to Mike and he can help you."

Wayne hit the tire iron against the side of the chair Libby was sitting in which caused her to flinch yet again but only served to make her madder. "What has he said about drugs in this area?"

Silent Rage

Libby slowly began to understand what was going on. She knew Mike was investigating some drug deals in Russell's neighborhood and even had a confidential informant. She didn't know who it was and didn't want to get that person in trouble. For all she knew it could even be Wayne. Libby figured she better tell Wayne something and maybe he'd let her go.

"All I know is there are a lot of drug deals in this neighborhood and the police are called out here a lot. Mike wants me to stay away but I have to check on my students."

"Mike is right. You need to stay away. So I'm gonna send him a message through you to keep out!" Wayne began to unzip his pants. Libby was frozen in terror of what might happen.

Wayne stepped closer and grabbed the back of her head causing her to look up. "Open up and make me feel good and I'll let you go." Libby was struggling and turning her head away but Wayne threw down the tire iron and used both hands to pull her head toward him. He rubbed her face in his crotch and Libby gagged on the smell of unwashed body and old sex. The next thing happened so fast Libby truly didn't know what hit her. She bit Wayne causing him to scream in pain. He reacted by hitting her across the cheek with his fist causing her head to snap in one direction and then he hit her again causing her to fall backward in her chair. Mercifully Libby passed out when she hit the floor and was unaware of what happened to her next. She did not feel the tire iron which slammed across her head or the kick in her ribs. She was unaware when he pulled down her pants and took advantage of her. When he was finished unleashing his rage he gave her a final kick and left without looking back. He didn't care if she rotted where she was. He wouldn't come back to free her, that was for sure. He had a drug enterprise to protect and that bitch was trouble. *Good riddance,* he thought.

"I'll send Bud to bury her," Wayne said to no one in particular.

Chapter 40
Mike

The divers were wading out of the pond and Mike was pacing back and forth on the edge of the water. When he saw them he started walking toward them, oblivious to the water he was stepping in to get there. "Well?" he asked.

The bigger of the two divers stepped headed for Mike. He briefly wondered how the man zipped his pot-belly into his dive suit. "There is not a body in that water. Plenty of other junk, but no bodies," the diver continued on past Mike to collect his gear and head out.

Mike let out a deep breath and mumbled, "Thank God."

Jump, however, was truly the bearer of bad news today. "Mike, there may be no body there but we've still got her abandoned car and we don't know where she is." He was trying to be cautiously optimistic with Mike while at the same time staying focused on the job at hand. It was not an easy task when emotions were involved. Jump liked Libby and hoped she would turn up safe and sound. "Let's go to the station and see if anything has turned up. Plus, I could use some coffee and some food and you need to eat to keep your strength up. Don't need you passing out from hunger."

"Fat chance of that. You, on the other hand, need constant food so I know it's really your own health you're worried about." Jump was glad to see Mike focus on something else at the moment and patted him on the back as the two walked to the car.

Chapter 41
Libby

Libby slowly opened her eyes and gave a moan at the pain she felt all over her body. It took her a moment to gather her wits and remember what happened to her. She could only open one eye since the other was swollen shut. She could tell her nose was most likely broken and felt what must be dried blood on her face. When she felt a breeze across her chest she attempted to lift her head and look but the pain to move was unbearable. Her side hurt like hell and her breasts felt like they were on fire. She would like to have pulled her blouse over her to cover herself but her hands were still tied behind her back and they both hurt as well. Probably from the fall and they might even be broken. Libby felt a tear trickle out of her one good eye.

"I will not give in to that bully!" Giving herself a mental pep talk, Libby tried to figure a way to get herself out of this mess. Moaning in pain she tried to roll over but it was pointless with all of her injuries. The only thing she could do at the moment was to pray for some divine intervention.

Libby could not begin to guess what time it was or how long she'd been missing and if anybody had even noticed yet. Giving a small sob she once again tried to right herself. She did not see the shadow pass the window. In her struggles she seemed to only be doing more harm than good to her injuries. She gave a scream of frustration. That was when she sensed someone else was with her. Ceasing all movements except for her eyes, Libby scanned the room to see who was there. Suddenly there was movement from the shadows and a dark figure ran over to where Libby was lying on the floor and bent to help her. Libby gasped in fear which quickly turned to surprise when she recognized the person.

"Russell! What are you doing here?" Libby was not quite sure what to think of this. Had Russell helped Wayne get her to this awful shed?

Russell took a moment to stare at Libby's open shirt and then pulled the sides together to attempt to cover her nakedness. Libby was grateful for the small act of kindness.

"Miss Teach, you've got to roll to the side so I can cut this tape binding you. Can you do that?" Russell was pushing Libby over on her face and causing her arms to strain even more. She gasped at the pain.

"I don't mean to hurt you but I've got to hurry and get you out of here before Wayne and his buddies return. I heard 'em talking about what they were gonna do to you and it'll be worse than what he's already done."

"How did you know I was here?"

As Russell cut away the thick tape binding her arms together he explained what happened.

"After you left my trailer I was watching you head back to your car. Mostly I was watching because it ain't safe around here after dark and I was worried you would get hurt. Turns out I was right to worry. I saw Wayne sneak up behind you and hit you over the head. Then he dragged you away. He doesn't like anyone he doesn't know nosing around his place. I started to follow him but when I got outside my door there was Bud and his gang waiting on me. They wouldn't let me leave. Said Wayne told 'em to babysit me until he got back. I was able to sneak away later but they caught me and this is the first chance I've had to come back and help you."

"How did you find me?" Libby was now able to move her arms but it was with terrible pain. Russell helped her get to a standing position. She pulled up her pants and shuddered thinking about how she felt and what Wayne must have done to her. It seemed like every part of her body was bruised or bleeding. Ironically she hoped all of the pain was from a beating because she didn't want to think what someone like Wayne would do to an unconscious woman. Her arms were tingling from the blood flow but Libby knew she couldn't give in to any pain now. Russell grabbed a couple of waters and told Libby to follow him.

"Where am I?" Libby asked again. After all of his chatting about how she was abducted it seemed now he wanted to be silent. She knew she needed a hospital but she also knew Russell most likely was a victim of abuse himself. If she could get him talking maybe she could figure out how to go about getting him away from Wayne.

"Wayne keeps this shed for his personal use."

"It looks like an old potting shed but I can't see him as a gardener."

Russell gave a bark of laughter that was not from happiness. "He uses it to satisfy his other needs. That's all I'm saying. Let's hurry before they all get back." With that Russell headed into the woods leaving Libby no choice but to follow him. She knew there was more to the story than he was admitting and she vowed she would find out somehow and help him. Thankfully her feet were ok and she could walk but she must have a broken rib or two because breathing was almost impossible.

Libby followed Russell through the woods. She was collecting more bumps and bruises and scrapes as they made their way through the thick foliage. She had no idea where they were going but Russell seemed in a hurry to get there.

"Where are we going?" Libby asked as she paused to catch her breath.

"I'm taking you to a place where there are people. After that I have to leave you and get back before he notices I'm gone," Russell called back over his shoulder but did not slow down.

"Wait up! How will get I home?" Libby started walking again and had tried to go faster just to stay within sight of Russell but the pain was unbearable. She held onto her ribs with both hands trying to ease the ache.

"You'll have to figure out getting home yourself. Maybe one of the people you see will be nice and help. I have to get back before Wayne notices I'm gone." Russell finally stopped and let Libby catch up. As she drew close he pointed to a place beyond the trees. "See that road through there? That is the main road before you turn down my street but it's way at the other end. You're not too near my road so you'll be safe from Wayne and the others who took you."

Libby looked through the branches and saw the road. "Yes, I see it. Are there any buildings nearby? I am not familiar with this area." But as she said it Russell took off in the opposite direction. "Russell! Don't leave me. I need a hospital!"

"Can't stay. You'll be ok, just head toward the setting sun." Russell headed deeper into the woods and

Libby felt more alone and vulnerable than she ever had in her life.

Libby looked back toward the road, took a deep breath, and began to walk out of the thick forest. She hoped and prayed a nice person was close by and would help her. When she finally made it to the road she realized how sore her feet felt but she kept on walking in spite of the blisters she knew were forming. She felt a sense of urgency to get as far away from Wayne as she could. She definitely didn't want to run into Wayne again.

Libby looked toward the sun to try and determine its position and get an idea of the direction and maybe even the time. As she looked up the movement reminded her of the massive headache she had thanks to getting clobbered. She thought she might even have a concussion. As long as she stayed awake and didn't get nauseous she thought she'd be fine. The staying awake part was easy since she was scared to death at the moment, but she did feel a little queasy. "Oh, please don't pass out." Libby said a little prayer and hoped the sickness would hurry and pass.

Heading down the road in the direction she hoped was west, Libby kept her eyes open for any passing motorists. She really wanted an elderly couple or even a grandmotherly lady to stop and help her. She wished she brought more water with her. She was incredibly thirsty. Was that a good or a bad thing for a concussion she wondered? She thought she heard a car approaching. She looked down the road and did see a vehicle coming at a pretty fast pace. She stood still and began waving her arms but the car was going so fast she didn't think the driver would see her because she wasn't close enough to the road. As it passed she noticed it was a police car. She began

Silent Rage

frantically waving and yelling but she didn't seem to get the officer's attention. The patrol car drove on without even touching the breaks.

"No! Stop! Idiot!" Libby watched in dismay as the black and white patrol car drove off without ever seeing her. At that moment she thought the car resembled a big panda bear running away. No wonder British crime shows called the cars pandas. Libby didn't know why her brain chose this particular moment to think about TV shows and cop cars. She thought to herself it was crazy what goes through the mind when it's put under stress. "Wait until I tell Mike about you!" But she knew it wouldn't matter. She didn't even know who was driving the car or if it was even in the right jurisdiction.

Libby took a deep breath and continued walking. "I will not get upset. I will not cry. I am going to get home very soon." Libby took a deep and painful breath as she began to made her way slowly down the road. It was an unusually warm day but that was better than being cold or wet. Time seemed to pass slowly and she thought she must surely be on the world's longest road. There was nothing in sight. Not a house, an abandoned trailer, or any kind of gas station. It was as if she was the only person in the world. Just then she heard the distinctive sound of a car coming her way.

"Finally! Hey! Over here!" Libby stepped into the road as the car neared and began waving her arms to get the driver's attention. For a minute she thought the car was just going to run her over and feared it might be Wayne coming to finish the job. At the last minute and with a squeal of brakes the car stopped.

"Crazy bitch! What are you doing out here?" The driver yelled out of her window.

"Oh please, I need help." Libby was saying as she made her way to the side of the car. It was then that she noticed the driver was Russell's mother. "Ms. Thomas, thank goodness. I was taking some school work to Russell and then Wayne hit me over the head and tied me up. Russell found me and helped me escape. You've got to get away from that man."

"You're crazy. Wayne wouldn't do that."

"Russell saw it. Do you doubt your own son?"

"He hates Wayne and always says lies about him. You must've had an accident and hurt your head and are just talking crazy. You look bad." Loretta was showing no signs of sympathy but in her head she knew what the teacher said was probably true. But what could she do about it? She needed a roof over her and Russell's heads and if she had to put up with Wayne then that's just the way it'd have to be.

"Please help me. I need to get to a hospital. I think I have a concussion and some broken ribs."

"I'll take you to the service station down the road and you can call EMS. That's all I've got time for so take it or leave it."

Libby didn't need to consider the offer she got right in the car and Loretta turned the car around and took Libby to the closest gas station. It was only about a mile down the road but Libby was thankful not to have had to walk that mile given her sore feet and other injuries.

Libby got out of the car and turned to say thanks but Loretta was already leaving the lot and heading back down the road.

Silent Rage

Chapter 42
Russell

Russell was upset that his favorite teacher and the only person who really seemed to care about him, was hurt so badly. He hoped she got to the hospital ok but he couldn't stay around to help her because he knew Wayne would be looking for him. However, something finally snapped inside Russell. He was tired of the sexual abuse Wayne meted out to him and he was going to do something about it. Wayne hurt his teacher and it was up to him to do something. He would get justice for her. As a matter of fact, as long as he was taking care of making things right, he would start with that counselor woman whose visits started all of this.

Russell quickly went to his secret place under the trailer and pulled out his newly acquired and prized possession. Wrapped in an old hand towel was a twelve-inch kabar knife with a leather handle. Russell knew it was similar to what Marines carried in the service but this knife didn't belong to any Marine. Russell had swiped it out of the back pocket of one of Bud's pals and the stupid guy never even felt it leave his pants. Russell also knew the knife was only worth about twenty bucks maybe a little more if you got it new but it would work just fine for what Russell planned to do with it. He wrapped the knife back up and stuck it in the waistband of his pants and headed into the woods.

Russell had not told his teacher about everything that went on in that awful shed. Wayne used it as a place to tie up Russell's hands and feet and then proceed to whip him with various objects and told Russell it was to drive the mean out of him. Russell knew Wayne was just psycho and liked to hurt people. He knew of another kid in the neighborhood he was willing to bet Wayne had abused too. Andy used to be nice to Russell but several months ago he quit coming over to hang out and he wouldn't even talk to him at school now. Russell figured Andy had been to the shed with Wayne. He got that idea when he saw Wayne coming out of the woods and looking all smug and happy and a few minutes later Russell saw Andy running out and heading toward his house. He knew there had been others too. Wayne used to pay some of the neighborhood kids five bucks to suck his dick in that shed. Russell knew this was true because he heard an older kid bragging about an easy way to get money.

Russell was feeling a lot of anger right now. He hated adults that took advantage of kids. He also hated adults who tattletale on kids and when they've finished they leave but then the parents hit them or in Russell's case, worse. He wandered through the woods and until he came to the school counselor's neighborhood and saw her house in the clearing. He snuck up to the window and looked inside.

I'll start with her. If she'd left us alone then Miss Teach wouldn't have had to come out and check on me, Russell thought.

Chapter 43
Margaret

Margaret Edwards sat in her den eating a dinner which consisted of a soy hamburger patty and steamed vegetables. The smell was unappetizing but she was trying to watch her calories and lower her cholesterol hopefully before she took her retirement cruise next summer. After thirty-five years with the school district she felt she had earned the trip and was very excited about her first trip abroad. Of course, it was just sailing the Caribbean for a week but she had never left the country and was eagerly anticipating the event. It was months away but that just meant she had time to get herself in a little better shape and who knows, maybe she would find a shipboard romance that could continue beyond the high seas.

Margaret was tired of the grind of the school. The amount of paperwork these days was enough to make anyone, and many did, quit the profession. Truth of the matter was she had once been a great elementary school teacher and loved all children. When she earned a degree in school guidance she had visions of helping lead students on paths to their greatest aspirations. Over time she had gotten bogged down in details, had seen may kids fall through the system, and met many deadbeat parents. One couldn't just say deadbeat dad anymore, there were plenty of awful moms out there too.

When the district office moved her to the middle school it began a slow death spiral for the once beloved teacher. She hated the older children and there were too many issues surrounding them. Parents were a pain in the neck to deal with and all the kids thought they were budding professional athletes. Whatever happened to a kid being a kid and simply playing outside or on neighborhood teams? Schools were requiring more and more from their staffs and it was no different for guidance counselors. She made personal visits to students and their families and hardly ever saw positive results. It was making her a very bitter person and that attitude carried over into her personal life.

In reality, it wasn't just the change in schools that made Margaret unhappy, it was the fact that she didn't have her own family to love and cherish. She would have enjoyed taking her own children to ballet lessons or soccer practice and she once had plans to do just that. Those hopes and dreams came to crashing halt when her fiancé and the love of her life was killed in a friendly fire incident many years ago. Margaret and her high school sweetheart, Stan Rollins, were engaged and planned to be married. Stan had joined the Army and was a helicopter pilot. The two planned to tour the world together on the Army's dime. They wanted to have at least four children and then grow old together and hopefully have lots of grandchildren. Those plans died when Stan's helicopter tragically crashed during training exercises. Margaret died that day too, at least her spirit did. Now many years later she hoped to find some joy in her retirement and the cruise was her lifeline to potentially happier days.

As she thought of Stan she couldn't help but think of their last time together. They were in her apartment enjoying a lazy Sunday afternoon cuddled together and content from their early morning love making. Margaret knew her parents would be appalled that she had slept with Stan before marriage. Their biggest fear would be for her to be a pregnant bride. *Times have sure changed,* thought Margaret. Now she is so glad that she and Stan had those magical and romantic moments together. The memories of those times were all she had to keep her warm these days. How Margaret wished things had turned out differently. She never did get pregnant and Stan was killed the following week. Her world changed and Margaret changed with it. She began the slow fall into the bitter and unloved old woman she is today.

With a sigh Margaret turned her thoughts toward contemplating her wardrobe for the cruise at the same moment when she heard a knock on her front door. She walked over to the door and peeped out of a side window and was surprised to see one of the students from the school where she worked standing on her porch.

"Russell, what are you doing here?" she asked as she opened the door.

"I heard your cat was missing and I found one in the woods over there but she's stuck or hurt or something. I don't know if it's your cat but I thought maybe you should go see."

"Oh, well thank you Russell but I doubt it is my cat because it's been a few weeks she went missing. I don't expect to find her at this point."

"But don't you wanna see just in case? It's a striped cat and I saw the missing signs and it looks like yours."

"I guess I could go take a look just in case it is my little Puff. That would certainly be a nice surprise to find her. I'll just get my sweater and you can show me." Margaret grabbed her sweater and then closed and locked her door. Even if she was just going around the corner she didn't want to leave her house unlocked for anyone to sneak in and rob her. She had to be careful since she was an older woman living alone.

Russell led the way to a path in the woods near her house. "Come on, she's over hear and she's probably hurt." Russell was more adept at maneuvering the dirt path than was Margaret. "Russell, I can't go over this ground as fast as you so slow down."

Russell turned to look at Ms. Edwards and said, "I'm doing this for your good so just come on. We're close."

Margaret grumbled but was hoping it was her Puff and that little damage had befallen her pet. The cat was all she had left in the world and she dearly missed it. She was so consumed with watching her steps that Margaret didn't notice Russell had disappeared. She suddenly realized she was lost and hadn't paid attention to where she was going. "Russell! Where are you? If this is some trick you're playing it is not at all funny!"

"This way." She heard Russell call from somewhere up ahead.

"I had no idea these woods were so deep. It's getting dark and I don't even hear a cat. Just take me back." Margaret heard something move in the bushes behind her and turned to see what it was. "I don't like this!"

"Well maybe I do!" Russell suddenly appeared in front of Margaret who jumped at the sound of his voice. "I've never liked you and I killed your dumb old cat."

"What? Why would you do that?" Margaret was starting to be very afraid of Russell. He seemed to have taken on a persona full of menace and evil.

"Because every time you came to my house after you left I was raped by that creep living there."

"I had no idea. Let me get you help now," Margaret begged.

"It's too late just like it's too late for you. I have plans for him but first I have to take care of you."

"What do you mean?" No sooner had she uttered the words than Russell waved a big knife in front of her. As she gasped and tried to take a step away, Russell quickly grabbed her by the arm and twisted her so that her neck was open toward the sky. He ran the knife across her neck and drew blood but the wound wasn't deep enough to kill her. This only enraged Russell. He let go of her and she grabbed her neck with both hands and fell to her knees. Seeing the old woman cowering before him filled Russell with a profound sense of power. He began stabbing her anywhere he could find to drive the knife deep into her body. She screamed and begged for him to stop but he was too caught up in his own type of feeding frenzy to hear her. His anger drove him like a madman and he eventually paused to take a breath. That's when he noticed there was no noise. The birds had stopped chirping, there were no insects singing their songs, and there certainly wasn't sound coming from the body at his feet. Russell took a moment to enjoy the ultimate power he had over the universe. He caused it all to stop just for him. He was in control.

As Russell slowly came out of his dark moment he took stock of the situation. He thought about what a soldier would do to an enemy he had killed and didn't want found right away. He looked around and saw a type of small hole in the side of a hill and under the roots of a big tree. He dragged her body over there and covered her with as much dirt as his hands could dig up along with some rocks and leaves. He looked at her and noticed her eyes were still open. Like they were looking into heaven or something. He hoped she was in hell because that's where she belonged and maybe she was even now having to do the nasty to the devil right now. Serves her right.

Russell took the rag out of his pocket and wiped off his knife. He didn't want her blood on his weapons. He looked at his own clothes and noticed how soiled they were. He was covered in the old woman's blood. He hadn't thought about bringing a change of clothes. It was his first kill and since he's only thirteen so surely no one would expect him to get it right the first time. He'd have to be more prepared when it was Wayne's turn to meet the devil. Lucky for him his mom was too high to ever notice anything about him and if Wayne said anything he'd just go ahead and kill him too. Wayne was next on his kill list. It wasn't a very long list. How many people could a thirteen-year-old want to kill anyway? He started whistling as he made his way home through the dark woods.

Chapter 44
Wayne

Russell entered the main room of his trailer and saw Wayne sitting on the couch wearing just his boxers.

"Where you been, boy? I had to get my own beer." Wayne gave a loud belch as if he was putting a smelly exclamation point on his words.

"I had to take care of something and it's about time you got your lazy butt up anyway." Russell was feeling a new sense of power after his previous adventure. He was no longer afraid of Wayne and in fact, he was going to take care of him once and for all right now. He slowly took the knife out of the waistband of his pants and dropped the rag that covered it. He held the knife behind his back and out of sight. He would show it to Wayne at just the right time.

"You retard! Don't you talk to me that way. I put a roof over your head and don't you forget it. As a matter of fact, I think it's time for you pay some rent," Wayne snarled through his yellowed teeth.

"Get over here, boy and make me feel like I should keep you and your no good momma around."

Something in Russell truly broke at the mention of his mother. "Shut up!" Russell charged toward him and plunged the knife deep into Wayne's neck. As he pulled it out blood spurted and covered Russell in the warm fluid. Russell looked at Wayne through a red haze and drove the knife into him over and over. Wayne was equally shocked and growing weaker by the minute. He was no match for the strength of the enraged, teenaged boy.

Russell lost all sense of time and his surroundings. When he paused to catch his breath he finally noticed

Wayne. The older man was a bloody mess slumped on the tattered sofa. There was so much blood it looked like someone had tried to dye the couch a hideous shade of red. Clearly Wayne would never demand payment from Russell or his mother again.

Chapter 45
Libby

Libby slowly opened her eyes and took in her surroundings. Mike, who was sitting beside her, stood up and called her name.

"Libby, are you finally awake?"

As she started to sit up she moaned at the pain that seemed to be in every part of her body.

"Don't try to sit up. I'll answer any questions you have and get you anything you need." Mike pulled her bandaged hand to his lips and gave her a gentle kiss.

"I'm thirsty." Libby's voice sounded hoarse even to her one ears. "What day is it?"

Mike poured some water into the cup by her bed and raised the straw to her lips allowing her to take a sip. "Go easy, you don't want to overdo it and throw up."

She laid her head back down and asked again, "What day is it? Did you catch him?"

"It's Tuesday. You've been in the hospital since Sunday night. Evidently you called for an ambulance from a gas station. They brought you in but you had passed out in the bus and they weren't sure who you were. When we got notice of a battered Jane Doe I came as quickly as I could to check it out. Just hoping and fearing it was you."

"My job." Libby was worried no one knew where she was and would assume she just went AWOL which would be a very bad thing in education.

"I called your principal and explained what was going on. Don't worry about your job. It's safe. They all send their best wishes and are taking care of your class for you. They sent all these flowers too."

Libby tried to turn her head but the movement caused too much pain. Mike noticed her grimace and volunteered to take pictures of everything from his phone. That way she could see without any extra movement.

"Now, while I'm showing you the pictures can you tell me what happened? All I know is you are pretty beat up." Mike got a little emotional when he said the words beat up.

"I went to see Russell." Libby then realized the predicament Russell might have faced when he returned home. "How is he?"

"Russell? Your student? He's fine as far as I know. Why are you worried about him?"

"His stepfather or whoever he is, his name is Wayne. He did this to me. If he found out Russell helped me escape, there's no telling what he might do to him."

"You're telling me your student's father beat you up?"

Libby explained how she went to take some school work to Russell since he was suspended. She described leaving and getting knocked unconscious and waking up in an old shed. She told Mike about the beating and how Russell rescued her and led her out of the woods. She also told Mike it was Loretta who gave her a ride to the service station and she remembers asking the attendant to call 911 and that's all she remembered until waking up a few minutes ago.

"Wow. So let me get this straight. It was this Wayne character who hit you and tied you up and then beat you?"

"Yes. He abuses Russell too. If he knows it was Russell who set me free there's no telling what he'll do to him. You've got to get Russell away from there."

"OK, I'll call it in and get someone sent over there."

"Mike, what did he do to me?" Libby asked as a tear rolled out of one of her bruised eyes.

"Oh honey." Mike kissed the top of her head and stroked her hair and comforted her.

"I bit him." Libby said between sobs.

"What?" Mike chuckled at that. "That sounds like my girl. How did that happen?"

"He wanted oral sex and I wasn't about to give in."

"Good for you but I'm not sure that was the best thing to do given the beating you received. He could've killed you."

"I think he probably thought I was dead. The last thing I remember is him raising the crowbar over me. I must have passed out then."

"You have a serious concussion and at least two huge knots on your head. Your nose is broken, your eyes are black and blue and one is swollen shut. You have three broken ribs, a broken wrist and the other is sprained. All in all, you are lucky to be alive. I can only imagine how you must feel."

"I actually don't feel too bad."

"Sugar, that's the medicine talking. You are so pumped full of pain killers and antibiotics. They've been keeping you sedated so your body can begin the healing process."

"Well, that explains it then." Libby gave a tired smile.

"I'm going to let you go back to sleep and I'll take care of getting Wayne arrested and Russell out of there." Mike gave Libby a very soft kiss on the lips and watched her close her eyes and immediately drift off to sleep.

Chapter 46
Essie

It was a full twenty-four hours since Libby talked with Mike and found out the extent of her injuries. She had slept most of that time and was finally feeling like she could sit up and stay awake long enough for visitors. Libby was glancing through a People magazine that one of the nurses had brought her when Essie peaked in the door and simultaneously gave a soft knock on it.

"Essie! Please come in."

"Oh sweetie, you poor thing." Essie went to give Libby a hug but couldn't decide where to touch her that wouldn't cause any pain. She decided a pat on the head and a friendly kiss on her forehead would have to suffice.

"Ouch!" Libby winced when Essie touched her head.

"I'm sorry! Oh gosh does your head hurt there too?"

"That must be one of the places he hit with me the crowbar. It's very tender and I think I have a matching one on the other side as well."

"He really did a number on you, didn't he?"

"Yes he did and I hope Mike has arrested him and he is locked away for life. He is evil. How bad do I look anyway?"

"You haven't seen yourself yet?" Essie asked with raised eyebrows.

"No, I've been out of it mostly. Can you bring me a mirror?"

"If you're sure you're ready for this. It isn't pretty."

"Gee thanks. And here I was thinking I must not look too bad after everything." Libby smiled to take the edge of her words.

Essie pulled out a pocket mirror from her large tote bag and held it up for Libby to see. Libby gave an involuntary gasp when she saw her black and blue face. She didn't look recognizable at all.

She emotionally said, "I could star in a Zombie show."

"You may look bad now but the body is a wonderful thing and you be back to your beautiful self in no time at all. Want to hear the latest news from school?"

"Yes. How are my students? Do they know what happened? Have you seen Russell?"

"I will answer all your questions just give me time." Essie chuckled. "First of all, yes your students know you were in an accident but they don't know all of the details. They made you a big card." Essie pulled the card out of her bag which made Libby think she looked like a magician pulling a rabbit out of a hat. "Here you go. All of your students designed and made the card during art class this week. They were very worried and glad to be able to let you know they missed you."

"This is so sweet. Please put it by the flowers so I can see it easily anytime I am feeling a little down."

Essie put the card by a big bouquet of fall colored wild flowers. Then she proceeded to tell her all the gossip from school.

"It seems we have a budding romance going on between one Miss Baker of P.E. fame and a Mr. Willis from the science wing."

"You're kidding? How nice for both of them. Neither one has ever been married and they've both been teaching about fifteen years, as far as I know." Libby liked both of the teachers and hoped they made a go of their relationship. "What else has been going on? It seems like months since I've been there rather than just a few days."

"I bet. Well, the oddest news is that Ms. Edwards is AWOL."

"What? That's not like her. She's counting down the days until her retirement next year. There's no way she would jeopardize that."

Essie told Libby that on Monday Ms. Edwards didn't report to work. No one thought much until about lunchtime when she still hadn't come in. The secretary called her home but didn't get an answer. Then she called the next of kin which was a distant cousin half way across the country and that lady hadn't heard from Ms. Edwards in years and was frankly, surprised to be listed as next of kin.

"The principal went out to Ms. Edwards' house but there was no sign of her anywhere and what was really odd was her car was in her garage. The principal looked through the cat door and saw the car parked. The district has sent a temporary counselor over until the mystery of Ms. Edwards is solved. Weird, huh?"

"Yes it is. I wonder if she went out walking and got hurt or something." Libby could relate to being stranded, in pain, and needing help. Maybe no one offered to help Ms. Edwards if that had happened to her.

The two friends talked a while longer when Essie remembered to tell Libby Russell hadn't been at school for a few days.

"Oh no. I hope Wayne didn't hurt him before Mike could arrest that loser." Libby was concerned that Wayne would inflict even worse damage on the young boy than he had on her and she wasn't sure what long term injuries that would cause for Russell.

"I'm sure he's ok." Essie changed the subject quickly so she wouldn't have to tell Libby what had happened while she was unconscious. After gossiping a while longer and hearing the latest details about Essie's love life, Essie could see Libby was tiring and gave her a tentative hug and assured her she would look after her apartment and her classes and visit her tomorrow. No sooner had Essie softly closed the door than Libby was fast asleep.

Chapter 47
Russell

While Libby had been unconscious, Russell had been going through an ordeal that would leave a permanent mark on his young psyche.

After the rage Russell experienced because of Wayne and which had resulted in Wayne's demise, Russell stood in the room in a state of mental confusion. Loretta finally came home from a night of partying and working. She opened the door to the trailer and walked into her own personal horror show starring her son. Russell stood covered in blood and holding a large knife which had clearly been used to end the life of Wayne. Loretta started screaming and couldn't stop. Russell dropped the knife and tried to get his mother to calm down but only succeeded in getting her covered in Wayne's blood. A neighbor heard the commotion and called the police.

When officers arrived on the scene they entered the mobile home and were greeted with what looked like a scene straight out of a Hollywood horror movie. Two figures stood before them covered in blood and clutching each other. A third bloody figure was not moving. One of the officers checked for a pulse and gave a shake of his head to his partner who was visually examining Loretta or Russell for injuries. Once it was determined Loretta and Russell were unharmed they were placed in handcuffs and put in the back of the squad car. One of the patrolmen radioed for help and crime scene investigators and detectives were on the way.

The coroner arrived and concurred it was a murder and stated the autopsy would reveal the exact fatal wound but a preliminary observation showed severe stabs to the neck and heart region any of which could've been fatal. The amount of blood led the coroner to surmise the jugular had been cut at some point during the attack.

Loretta and Russell were taken to the precinct and placed in separate rooms. A child advocate was called in for Russell, who refused to talk until he could see his mother and know she was ok. Once he was assured she was nearby and doing fine, he slowly began to relax and relate the events that described the horror of his youth.

"So Russell, you freely admit to killing Wayne Turner?" asked Detective Raymond Smith. Smith was chosen for the interview because of his calm demeanor and knowledge of the area Russell called home.

"Yes. He deserved it for what he did to my mom and to me," Russell answered.

Russell also was able to maintain eye contact with Raymond which made the seasoned detective a little unnerved since he expected the youth to be scared and nervous.

"You want to tell me a little about that?" asked Raymond.

"Russell, you don't have to talk about anything that makes you uncomfortable. We can talk about what happened before today whenever you're ready and we can even go to a more relaxing room." This was spoken by Russell's child advocate. Ann Johnson was a no nonsense professional. In her mid-forties, she was still slim and attractive and kept her dark blonde hair cut in a shoulder length bob. Everyone had great respect for her and knew she had the interests of the child at heart. Whenever she intervened or cut short an interview it was because she sensed the child was having trouble with the situation. Law enforcement personnel trusted her instincts and adhered to her direction with troubled youths thus allowing for a very good working relationship. Both sides were happy whenever the case belonged to Ann.

"I don't mind talking," Russell interjected.

Ann spoke up again, "Are you sure? Can we get you a soda or anything?"

"I'd like a coke, please."

Ann nodded to an officer who stepped out of the room to retrieve a cold soda for the troubled youth. He returned and placed the can in front of Russell who immediately opened it and took a long drink.

"Russell, you ready to tell us how you got to be in that trailer holding the knife over Wayne?" Raymond began the interrogation.

"I killed him."

"Now Russell, don't admit to anything just to protect your mom."

"I'm not. I killed him."

Raymond was skeptical and looked at Ann who nodded it was ok to continue.

"Tell me how you did that."

"I used my kabar knife. I keep one for hunting and I always have it with me. Except, of course, at school. They'd expel me if I brought a weapon to school. I take good care of my knife. I want to be a soldier one day and carry a real one."

"You're interested in knives then are you?" Raymond inquired.

"Yes sir. I like to use them when I go hunting and skin the animals I kill. I've gotten pretty good at it."

211

Silent Rage

This was troubling news to the professionals in the room. A young boy who has suffered abuse and now kills small animals sent major red flags to the behavioral psychologists and law enforcement personnel listening in from another room. The fear was these were the beginning traits of a budding serial killer. Ann would now have to determine how much damage Russell had suffered and what kind of psychiatric treatment he would require. At this point in the interview a silent signal took place between Raymond and Ann and Ann took over the questioning and gently prodded Russell into revealing some of the horrific things he experienced during his childhood.

"Russell tell me what it was like when you were younger and it was just you and your mother," asked Ann.

"I don't really remember a time like that. We've always lived in that mobile home and there was always some guy living with us. Wayne's been there the longest."

"How did Wayne treat you?"

Russell was looking at his hands which were clinched in fists. He took so long to answer Ann was about to rephrase the question when Russell started to speak.

"Wayne used to hit me when my mom wasn't around. He liked to hit me on the head and he could hit pretty hard too. It's like I always had a headache."

"So Wayne was physically abusive to you, is that right?" Ann was trying to establish a consistent life of abuse so that the courts would take that into consideration with Russell's sentence.

"Yeah and he pushed me a lot too. I think he did that 'cause I'm smaller than him and he could get away with it."

Did he ever hit you in public?" Ann asked.

"Sometimes in the yard at home when he was trying to show off in front of the other guys in the neighborhood. Mostly he did things to me inside when my mom was at work."

"I'm so sorry you had to go through all that Russell. So along with the physical abuse did Wayne say things to you that made you feel bad?"

"He liked to call me retard. It always embarrassed me when he did and other people could hear him."

Russell continued relating the details of his sad existence in a monotone.

"Russell, do you have any other family members that you will be able to stay with one you are away from here?" Ann didn't know how long Russell would remain in custody and she needed to find somewhere for him to stay in case he is released soon.

"It's always just been me and my mom. I don't have any other family. My mom got pregnant when she was a teenager and her mom threw her out of the house. I don't know anything about her mom, not even her name." Raymond thought to himself it would be a fairly easy thing to find out who Loretta Thomas' mother was and he signaled for a uniformed officer to get busy looking into that. If Loretta has any responsibility in the murder of Wayne, then Russell was going to need somewhere to stay.

"What about your dad? Do you know where he is?" Ann kept the interview moving along.

"My mom would never tell me. Says she loved me enough and I didn't need anyone else. But one time she told me his name was Roger and he was dead so I didn't need to go trying to find him or anything."

"She didn't tell you anything else about him like where he lived?" Studies showed that people who survived traumatic situations had a better chance of recovery when there was a strong family support system. If she could find a means to establish a family connection it might go a long way in helping Russell to get the treatment he needed to be able to live a relatively normal adult life. At least that was what Ann hoped.

Just then Raymond's partner, Detective Wilson stuck his head in the door and motioned he needed to speak with Raymond. "How about we take a little break and Russell if you need a soda or a bathroom break the officer in the hallway here, will take care of you. I'll be back shortly."

Ann and Russell sat back in their chairs as Raymond went out the door.

Once in the hallway Raymond asked, "What's up?"

"Loretta just lawyered up. Burns showed up," Al explained.

"What? She's got that expensive prick as a lawyer? How can she afford his rates?" Raymond was starting to get concerned this might not be the open and shut case it first appeared to be.

Gregory Daniel Burns III was a typical gangster lawyer. He was born into a family dynasty that had been bailing out and representing the criminals of society for over three generations. They had made a substantial amount of money from it so it was naturally assumed young Gregory would enter the family business. He did and he loved every minute of it. He didn't care that his clients were all as guilty of their crimes as Cain was of slaying Abel. More than representing the scumbags, he enjoyed the

214

enormous fees they paid him just to be on call for them. He also got quite a few perks out of it as well. One such perk was now parked outside of the station. It was the latest model of a fully loaded Mercedes Benz which he had handpicked on a trip to Germany and had it shipped directly to his house. Ironically, Burns was an excellent lawyer and would've made a fortune no matter which path in the legal profession he had chosen. Needless to say, the police were not big fans of his.

"Turns out she works at Sassy A's and her boss sent his minion over to take care of her."

"Damn, what's up with that? He must really like Loretta. I've never know Sam Dawkins to care about anyone other than his own sorry ass."

"Says he's gonna take care of the boy too."

"Well, not much he's going to be able to do since the kid admits he did it and we got his prints all over the knife." Raymond was beginning to get a headache and as much as he hated for a child to be incarcerated it might be the most stable place a kid like Russell ever lived. He just hoped the system could really help Russell. He doubted it though.

Chapter 48
Russell

Russell looked up at the tall and handsome man who entered the room. He was wearing a dark suit with a red tie and Russell noted the little flag on his lapel. In Russell's mind he looked like an actor from that show his mom watches about Mafia gangsters.

"Who are you?" Russell asked the man.

"Hello, Russell." Burns stuck his hand out to shake Russell's. "Name is Greg Burns and I am going to make sure you are treated right and get the help you need."

Burns sat down opposite Russell. "Don't say anything else and make sure I am with you before you even ask for a glass of water. You got that?"

Russell nodded. "I asked for a coke, was that ok?"

"No worries, I'll take care of it."

For the next hour Burns detailed all he was going to do for Russell and how if Russell did all Burns directed him to do then he would simply spend a few years in a juvenile detention center and once he was eighteen he would be free to go back into society and pursue whatever hopes and dreams he had.

"I want to join the Army." Russell spoke up after he realized he might still be able to do that.

"That's a good goal. You study and do the things required of you at the center and you'll be fit and ready for the Army on your eighteenth birthday." Burns didn't tell him it would be an uphill battle but he would do what he could to get Russell's record clean.

Russell finally smiled. It was a genuine smile that lit up the young boy's face. Burns sort of felt sorry for the boy and determined he would do everything in his power to help the kid get to the Army.

Chapter 49
Loretta

Over the next several weeks the investigation discovered Russell had been the one holding the knife that ended Wayne's life. Loretta had come home to find her son in a crazed fog after stabbing Wayne. She did what any mother would naturally do when she found her son had killed her lover and that was start to screaming and hold onto her son. This explained the blood on Loretta. What they couldn't explain were the traces of another blood type not related to the crime scene. It didn't match Wayne's, Loretta's, or Russell's. The detectives and criminologists on the case decided it must have been something that was already on the knife, maybe a cut from a previous owner. They didn't investigate any further, confident they had closed the case on the Wayne Jetsoe murder.

Loretta was cleared of charges and went back to her life of booze, drugs, and stripping. She visited her son regularly at the juvenile detention center where he had been remanded after being charged with Wayne's murder. He was currently in the middle of the court proceedings. His attorney was claiming he was guilty but with extenuating circumstances due to his fear for his life. Most of the people who came into contact took a liking to the quiet and polite young man.

Russell was actually more relaxed than he had ever been in his young life. This was most likely because he was no longer getting abused by Wayne and he had access to regular meals and a shower. No one knew what kind of trouble was waiting down the road for the young killer, but for now Russell seemed oddly happy. His lawyer kept his word and had done a good job getting charges reduced for his young client. All parties had agreed to a bench trial and as luck would have it, Russell appeared before a judge who was sympathetic to youthful offenders. Judge Anthony Carlson wanted to give Russell an opportunity at a normal adult life so he sentenced him to five years in the juvenile center along with mandatory counseling. It was a win-win situation. The city was glad to have the case closed and a perpetrator sentenced. Russell would be free and clear to potentially join the Army once he turned eighteen. Even now his lawyer was working on getting his record erased so there would not be any hurdles into joining the military for Russell.

Chapter 50
Mike

It was a rough several days for Mike. When Libby turned up missing his heart practically stopped beating. He couldn't imagine a life without her. Thankfully she turned up alive and was on her way to healing. Her recovery would be a slow process and one filled with some psychological scars as well. Mike planned to be with Libby every step of the way and help her get back to her spunky self.

In the meantime, Mike had to deal with the fallout from the shootings at Sassy A as well as the Flowers Farm drug sales. Albert Moore was gunned down by one of the Flowers men. Dalbert was so consumed with grief for his twin that he was willing to tell the police everything he knew about Sassy A, drugs, and the murder of his twin.

Raymond Smith questioned Albert. "We know Sassy A was into some drug deals. How about you tell us who was selling for you and where you got the merchandise to begin with."

"Anything I tell you is gonna help you fry the guys that killed my brother right?" Albert wanted to know.

"That's right. Every little detail you give us is just more evidence that will nail them." Raymond couldn't believe Albert wasn't asking for a deal for himself. The guy must not know he's in trouble too. *What an idiot.* "So tell me who took the product off your hands?"

"Lucky Sam had about three guys who took it to the street."

"Names?"

"The only one whose real name I know is Bud and only 'cause he's the dishwasher at Sassy A."

"What do you know about the other two? I can't believe you don't have a way of contacting them."

"You didn't ask me that. Only if I knew their names."

"Well, how do you get in touch with them then?"

"I call 'em."

"Your momma must've dropped you on your head when you were a baby."

"You leave my momma out of this," yelled Albert.

"OK, so listen real careful and I'll say it real slow so you can understand."

"'K."

"What is the number of the two guys you call to sell your drugs and what name do they go by? Is that simple enough for you, moron?" Raymond was losing his patience with Albert.

"I don't know the number I just push the button for whichever one I want."

"You are one dumb SOB."

"Hey, I said…"

"I know, I know. Leave your momma out of it. So just show me on your phone which number and name you push to get the two guys you need." Raymond pulled Albert's cell phone out of a box that was on the table in the interview room. He handed the phone to Albert.

"So Jax is one of the guys and this is his number." Albert showed Raymond the display and he made note of the first number.

"You call him Jax? Don't have any more names for him?"

221

"No. The other guy is Hoops on account of he played basketball when he was in high school. He was pretty good too."

Raymond now had the names and cell phone numbers of the two guys Lucky Sam used to hawk his product on the street.

"I can get in touch with Bud at the club but have you got a number for him too?"

"No, cause we always talked to him at work. So you ain't asked me about the shooting. You need to arrest them."

"We are already in the process of bringing them in. We got a witness that caught their tag number when they drove away. Saw the shooting and everything. Now we just need these three scum bag drug dealers and we can close this case," Raymond informed Albert.

"So you going to charge them Flowers boys with murder?" asked Albert.

"Sure are. Just like I'm going to charge you with murdering their brothers."

"What? I thought we were just getting evidence against them Flowers boys."

"Interesting you should know it's the Flowers boys we've got in the other interview room."

"Why?"

"I never told you who was driving the truck and you told me you didn't see the shooters. If you didn't see them how do you know it was the Flowers guys?" asked Raymond.

"They was always giving us trouble 'cause they were trying to take over our customers. Even had guys bring some of their blow into Sassy A. Lucky Sam didn't like that."

Raymond couldn't believe this guy was just willingly giving him so much information. The guy had even waived his right to an attorney. What a win for the war against drugs in their little neck of the woods. "So what did Lucky Sam do about this invasion of his turf?"

"He told me and Dalbert to go teach 'em a lesson."

"So is this when you go over to their place and start shooting any members of the Flowers family you two see?"

Albert hesitated, "I'm starting to think I might need a lawyer after all. I don't want Lucky Sam mad at me or nothing."

"You don't need to worry about him. We've got him taken care of." Lucky Sam was currently sitting in a jail cell waiting on his turn with the detective.

"I don't know. Maybe I just better quit talking now."

"Suit yourself." Raymond picked up the cell phone from the table and put it back in the box. Taking the box with him, Raymond told Albert to sit tight and left the room.

The eyewitness to the shooting at Sassy A had provided the license plate number of the truck to the police. The plates were run and the names given led them straight to Candie's Acres of Flowers and the remaining two men in the Flowers family. As the old saying goes, "if it weren't for bad luck they'd have no luck at all" summed up the miserable existence of Timmy and Butch Flowers. When Mike and Jump arrived at the farm to question the men about the use of their truck in the recent shooting at Sassy A, they saw the vehicle in question parked right in front of the house. The doors were open as if the truck needed airing out. The officers calmly walked over to inspect the truck and discovered bullet casings on the floor of the vehicle. Just as one of the detectives reached with his pencil to get a casing and put it in a plastic bag, shots were fired in their direction. The men ducked behind the car and aimed their weapons in the direction of the gunfire.

"Police! Put down your weapons," Mike said.

"This is private property and you need to leave," said Timmy Flowers.

"We aren't going anywhere without you and your brother. We even got a warrant for your arrest."

"What for?" asked Butch Flowers.

"Seems you two have been shooting up some fine business establishments and killed one of the workers."

"We did not. We didn't even aim at anyone," said Timmy.

"Shut up you moron," said Butch.

The two officers looked at each other and just grinned and shook their heads. If only all criminals were so talkative.

"This is your last chance. Put your weapons down and come out with your hands up. I'm sure your mom doesn't want dead bodies littering up her place," said Jump.

The Flowers boys looked at each other and then came to an unspoken agreement that it was better to be alive and in prison than dead. They put their weapons on the ground, raised their hands, and walked toward the officers.

"Stop right there," Jump yelled.

The two brothers stopped walking but kept their hands up.

"Slowly get on your knees." Mike and Jump left the shelter of the truck.

"No sudden moves or a bullet will be the last thing you feel," said Jump.

Mike holstered his gun and proceeded to handcuff the Flowers men.

Once they were secured Mike and Jump each took a brother and pulled him to his feet.

"Come on. You're getting in the back of the car," Mike said as he gave a shove to Timmy.

"Hey, that's police brutality," Timmy complained.

"That ain't nothing, you wuss," Jump said as he gave Butch a rough push into the back of the patrol car. Butch caught his head on the top of the car as he fell into the seat.

"Damn, that hurt."

"Quit complaining. You two don't need to be acting like ladies before you even get to prison. Show a little pride and play hard to get to all the cons you'll be living with." Jump laughed at his own comment.

"Let's call it in and get a crime scene team out here to look at this truck," Mike said.

The two officers got in the car and made the call then took the Flowers boys in to be processed.

Chapter 51
Candie

Candie Flowers was hiding behind a curtain and watching the scene being played out in her front yard. She was so mad she couldn't think straight. She let the curtains fall close and went to the kitchen to pour herself a cup of coffee. She poured some bourbon in and drank it all in one long gulp. She slammed the cup on the counter and went into her office to look at the state of her business. She was having to do everything these days since all her sons were either missing or were going to be in prison for the foreseeable future. *Those boys better not bring me into it,* she thought.

It didn't seem like any time had passed when she heard a car in the driveway and the closing of two doors.

They can't be out already. Candie went to the same window she had looked out of earlier and saw the same two police officers heading up her front steps.

Mike gave the door a couple of hard knocks. When no one answered Jump knocked more firmly on the door and yelled, "Open up!"

Candie gave a loud sigh and yanked open the door. "What do you want? I ain't got any more sons for you to arrest. Maye a daughter-in-law I'd like to get rid of but no men."

"Ma'am, we aren't here for any male members of your family," said Mike.

"We aren't looking for your daughter-in-law either," Jump added.

"Well you ought to be. Her name is Missy and she's trouble." Candie figured she could send the officers on a

226

wild goose chase. Truth was she had no idea where Missy had run off to.

"We are here to speak with you, ma'am," Mike said.

"Me? What the hell you want with me?"

"On the way to the station to process your sons they had quite a lot to talk about while they were in the back of the car. I'm not sure they realized we could hear everything they said."

"Those idiots. They're dumber than a jackass and that's an insult to the animal."

Mike and Jump again looked at each other.

"We're not here to discuss their IQ's. We need to take you with us down to the station," Mike said.

"What for? They can't need bailing out already."

"No ma'am they do not. But we do need to ask you some questions about recent events at your place of business," Jump said.

"My business ain't no business of yours," Candie said.

"We can sort that out at the station. You can come willingly or I can be of assistance in getting you to the car," Jump said. He was hoping she needed his help. He would gladly place this sorry woman in handcuffs and put her in the patrol car.

"What do you need me to talk about? I can answer any questions right here."

Mike spoke up, "Your sons were discussing some, what you might call business associates, and the word cocaine kept coming up."

"Look officer, we sell flowers. Maybe you just misunderstood and he was talking about some of our seeds we sell."

"I'm pretty sure my hearing is just fine and I believe it was Timmy who said you had a little sideline of selling cocaine and meth."

Candie looked thoroughly disgusted with her sons, herself, and the current predicament she was placed in due to her loudmouth boys talking too much. *If prison doesn't kill them I will,* she thought.

"I just got one word for you—lawyer," Candie said.

"That's fine with us Ms. Flowers but you still have to come along for a ride and you can call your lawyer once we get you nice and settled in," Jump said.

"Let's go," Mike said as he grabbed Candie by the arm and gently pulled her toward the patrol car.

"I can take myself to the car," Candie said as she jerked her arm away from Mike's grasp. "I don't trust you not to 'accidentally' push my face into the door of the car," Candie said putting finger quotations around the word accidentally.

The three of them made their way to the car. Candie was put in the backseat without any incident. The ride to the station house was done in relative quiet. Once there she was put in a conference room to await her turn talking with a detective. They were going to let her sit a good while and get her uncomfortable and needing a bathroom break. That way she would probably provide them with information just so she could escape and relieve herself. The Flowers family matriarch was not going anywhere soon.

Silent Rage

Missy Flowers was miles away from Candies' Acres of Flowers. She had escaped Candie's clutches a few weeks ago when trouble first started happening at the farm. Her husband had gone missing and no one seemed to know where he was. Missy knew Candie didn't like her and suspected her son had run off with some money and was in hiding waiting for Missy to join him. Candie had accused her of making Hank steal from his family. Missy could still recall the heated conversation.

"I know you forced Hank to steal some money from me," Candie said

"I did no such thing. You don't trust anyone and you treat your family like they're worthless trash. Maybe they got together behind your back and plotted to keep the money away from your greedy hands," Missy yelled at Candie.

Candie reached out and slapped Missy across the face. "My boys love me and wouldn't ever betray me. You, on the other hand, are nothing but a pain in everyone's ass. Always complaining and putting on airs like you're better than everyone. That husband of yours has had a woman on the side since about the day you said I do. I have no idea why he ever married you."

Missy was holding her face where she could still feel the imprint of Candie's hand. "You are a despicable person. You can't tolerate the fact your sons might want to get away from you. I can't stand to be anywhere near you and I'm getting out of here today. I hope one day your evil ways catch up with you and you rot in prison."

"Fat chance of that," Candie said.

Missy spent the rest of that afternoon packing her clothes and reviewing her plans. She wished she knew where Hank was. He'd been gone a while now and she couldn't imagine what had become of him because she knew he liked his life on the farm and had no plans of ever leaving it or his momma. Missy begged Hank on numerous occasions to take her away and start their own business and leave the mess that was going on at Candie's Acres of Flowers. Hank didn't know how she knew but he told her he was too used to the money the drugs brought and he had no plans of changing his lifestyle.

Missy couldn't believe Hank wouldn't leave with her but he simply told her she could be replaced and no one would ever question her absence. That comment actually scared Missy and so she began to make arrangements to sneak away from the Flowers family and go somewhere safe.

Chapter 52
Libby

It has been three weeks since the case against Russell was resolved and he was moved to the state juvenile detention center where the most serious of young offenders served their sentences. Libby was making the trip to visit Russell for the first time. She felt a bond with the boy since he was the one who rescued her from the shed and from what most likely would have turned out to be a fatal event for her. She carried with her a few magazines about the military to give him along with a book about military history in the United States. She hoped it was within protocol to give him the gifts. She had checked with the sheriff and he felt confident she could give him those items.

Libby carefully read the dress code for visitations. She was all set in her black slacks and long sleeved maroon blouse that she specifically bought one size larger so that it would not be thought of as clingy. She even had on a new pair of flats just to make sure that no part of her outfit was thought of as sexual. She couldn't believe some of the items that had to be listed as not allowed. Fish net shirts, really? What were some people thinking?

Libby smiled over at Mike and placed her hand on his knee. He wanted to accompany her on this visit. After her ordeal, Mike was still reluctant to let Libby out of his sight for long.

"Thanks for coming with me."

"You know I wouldn't let you do this alone." Mike was enjoying driving the TR6 and shifted gears to go a bit faster on the long stretch of highway.

"I know but I also know you are right in the middle of a few renovations at the new house and taking a free Saturday off is quite a sacrifice for you." Libby worried Mike was spending too much time with her and not enough on the remodeling. She just didn't want to be a burden to him.

"I am making good progress on it and besides, Jump volunteered to do some painting for me today."

"Wow. That's nice but I bet his wife isn't happy about that."

"Au contraire, ma cherie. She is very glad he is out of the house because he took William, his sixteen-year-old. Evidently William is quite the mouthy teenager these days and Jump is making him do some manual labor as a way to work on his attitude." Mike gave a chuckle.

Libby also laughed. "Well, that certainly puts a new light on things. I am glad they are doing something to work on William's attitude. These days' youths and even younger kids are so full of themselves with their big mouths and even bigger talk. They really do have crappy attitudes and think 'it's all about them'." Libby could go on a tirade about the way today's kids acted. Mike knew to change the subject or he'd be dealing with a tense woman. He wanted to have a good time and get her to relax. He knew the detention center was always a stressful place to visit and this was going to be Libby's first visit seeing Russell there.

"So tell me about the books you got for Russell." Mike tactfully changed the subject.

Libby took a calming breath and looked at the books she held in her lap.

"I thought Russell would like to read some military stories so I bought a couple of age appropriate books for him."

"From what you've told me about him I bet they become his favorite books."

They continued the drive and talked about many things including the plans for the new house. The detention center was about two hours away and the couple enjoyed the uninterrupted time together.

They stopped talking when the detention center came into view. They simply stared at the imposing complex. The sprawling place appeared to have at least ten and possibly even more buildings toward the rear of the property. The cell houses were made of concrete block and brick and laid out in such a pattern that it appeared as if the structures themselves wore prison stripes of brown and red. Observers immediately knew something serious was behind the razor wire atop the twenty-foot fencing. In a nearby area there was a second row of razor wire just a few feet before a tall concrete block wall. There was a guard tower in one area of the wall.

Mike was looking at the unusual fencing and wall and decided it must be where the juvenile offenders got to enjoy some recreation time. He pointed to it and said, "Hear the voices over there?"

"Yes," Libby replied as she looked to where Mike was pointing.

"That's most likely the recreation yard. I wonder how big it actually is and what they get to do in it?"

"Yeah, me too. But it still seems very sad. You've got to wonder what drove these youths to be such violent offenders and what could've been done to prevent it."

"Sweet pea, it sounds like you're already trying to psychoanalyze them." Mike teased her.

"Well, one day I will be doing something just like that. I've only to get that Masters finished and then I can see if I need a PhD." Libby enjoyed her research on juvenile criminals and hoped to someday be able to work with them in a more productive way.

Mike parked the car and he and Libby made their way to the front of the building.

"Are you ready for this?" Mike asked as he held open the door to the visitors' area for Libby.

"As I'll ever be." Libby took a deep breath and clutched the magazines and books to her chest as she entered the lobby.

Mike led the way to the officer on duty's desk to begin the check-in process.

"Good morning, officer. We are here to see Russell Thomas and we should be on the approved visitor list." Mike was already handing his badge and gun over to the officer. Libby had her wallet out as well.

Officer Manny Cortez took the items from Mike and placed them in a lock box that he catalogued and put in a slide through drawer that disappeared into a room beyond prying eyes.

"Happy to have you visiting us and just so you know, your weapon and badge are put back there in a locked room. You'll obviously get them back when you leave. Ma'am I need to see those books you've got there along with that folder."

Libby stepped up and placed the book and magazines on the table. Officer Cortez took them and ran a hand scanner of some sort over them and then gave each item a shaking in order to dislodge anything stuffed inside.

"Just checking for anything that shouldn't be in the book. Not that I think you'd sneak in drugs or a weapon but I have to follow procedure." Officer Cortez handed the materials back to Libby and then pushed a switch that would open the metal door leading to another waiting area.

Once Mike and Libby had passed through the initial check-in they were then led to a room where a couple of dogs sat attentively beside another officer. The animals were intimidating in size, as they were clearly pure bred German Shepherds. Their ears were alert but their eyes were on the officer. He gave a command to them and they each sniffed Mike and Libby.

"This is unsettling." Libby was nervous and hoped the dogs didn't alert that something was wrong with her.

"Just procedure ma'am. We have the dogs smell everyone. You'd be surprised what some people try to sneak in and even more surprised where they put it."

Mike snorted. "I can imagine."

The officer allowed them to pass and they were then escorted into a large room that was obviously a type of meeting room for visitors and inmates. They scanned the room looking for Russell and saw him sitting in a corner by himself. He looked as if he had shrunk since the last time Libby had seen him.

She whispered to Mike, "let me do the talking and don't say anything about my conversation until we leave."

Mike thought the request was strange but he went along with it.

Libby smiled and waved at Russell as she walked across the room. He saw her approaching and gave her a shy smile.

"Hi, Miss Teach. It's nice to see you. I was glad when they told me you were visiting 'cause I knew you were ok. I hadn't heard much before."

"I'm glad to see you too Russell. I'm sorry they didn't keep you informed about me. I am still very grateful for your help in getting me out of that shed."

"I hope they burned that place down." Russell mumbled this as he bent his head down. Libby couldn't help but notice that Russell was still a shy and withdrawn youth. She hoped her visits, and she did plan more, would let Russell know that there were people who cared about him.

"It seems we both have bad memories of that place. Maybe someday we can swap stories. But first, do you remember Officer O'Malley?"

"Yes. I remember he was at the trailer when they came because of Wayne."

"Right. Well, he also happens to be my fiancé and he wanted to come with me today when I met with you. He is going to sit over there on that sofa while we have a chat. Is that ok with you?" Libby pointed to a nearby sofa that was close enough for Mike to help her if for any reason she needed it but at the same time was far enough away to afford a feeling of privacy to Russell.

Mike gave a little wave to Russell and then walked over to the sofa, picked up a random magazine on the side table, and took a seat.

Russell watched Mike the entire time and then looked back at Libby. "You're gonna' marry him?"

236

"Yes. In just a few more months my name will be Mrs. O'Malley. You can still call me Miss Teach though, if that's easier for you."

"I like Miss Teach 'cause you're a teacher."

"I think most students feel the same way that you do." Libby gave Russell a smile as she said this.

"Russell there is something that I'd like to ask you. It's sort of a favor to me."

"OK."

"You may have heard me mention in class sometime that I am working on a Master's degree. I've always told my students I am a student too so I understand the demands life puts on all of us when it comes to completing assignments. Do you remember me talking about that?"

"Yes ma'am."

"Good. That brings me to the question I have for you."

Mike had been half listening to Libby but something in her tone caught his attention and he began listening more closely to what she was saying.

Libby continued talking to Russell, "One of the courses I am taking requires me to do a research project on a juvenile who has gotten into some trouble." She didn't want to call Russell a delinquent but the assignment called for research on a convicted juvenile delinquent. "The research would require me to make multiple visits with you and for you to tell me all about your childhood and whatever family life and other relatives you can remember and want to share with me. Would you be agreeable to being the subject of my research project?"

Mike was getting a little concerned with this project and wondered just how much time it would take for Libby to make several visits out to the center to gather all the information she would need for the project.

Russell replied, "Does that mean you would have to come see me a lot and all I have to do is tell you about me?"

"Pretty much, yes."

"Then I want to help you with your project," Russell answered eagerly.

Libby smiled. "That's wonderful Russell. I'll take care of the paperwork that allows you to talk to me. I do have a form you sign that says you agree to me asking you questions and if you want we can get started today."

Mike just stared at Libby. He had not expected this to be a working visit. He was a little nervous about her spending so much time with a convicted murderer even if the guy was a young teenager.

Libby pulled a form out of the file folder she brought and slid the paper to Russell. It explained the research process to him.

"At some point I will start writing down the things you tell me just so I remember them correctly. But today, let's just talk and enjoy the visit."

"OK." Russell actually looked a little happier now that he was going to be seeing more of Miss Teach.

"Great. Now let's just start with some basic information. You can tell me what you know about where you born and any other family members besides your mom."

"I was born back in town. I've never been anywhere else, until now. My mom didn't have any money for vacations and she was always working anyway."

"Vacations can be expensive. I got your birthday from your school records but I don't have your father's name. Do you know what his name is?"

"My mom wouldn't ever tell me who he was. She always said I was better off not knowing. But I found a piece of paper in her dresser drawer one day. It was stuck in this little blue Bible that had my name and my parents' names on it. I still have 'em both 'cause I put it in my backpack and they let me keep it with me here."

"OK, so is it a birth certificate or something?"

"No it's a newspaper article but it's about the man she wrote is my daddy in the little blue Bible."

"Do you have it with you now?"

"Yes ma'am. If I leave my stuff alone the other guys in here would steal it so I always carry my backpack with me." Russell leaned over and pulled out the small Bible. He then opened it up to the first page with his family tree written on it. He gave the Bible and the article to Libby.

The first thing Libby saw was a small notation most likely written by Russell's mother. It said: "In case you ever need to know your dad for medical reasons." Libby thought that was interesting and at least his mom had left a way for Russell to find his family. Maybe when he got out of the center he could live with his father. Libby planned to find out where the man was. Next she unfolded the newspaper clipping and read the title: "Convicted killer executed!"

Silent Rage

Libby stifled a gasp as she read the headlines and she thought poor Russell didn't get any breaks. Next she read the first line of the article and her blood ran cold. She quickly grabbed the Bible and looked at the name on the line for father. There it was—Roger Allen Watson. Her uncle, the killer's father.

Russell looked deep into the eyes of his teacher and asked, "Do you think I'll grow up to be like him?"

Libby was still in shock after reading that her uncle was also Russell's father. That made Russell her cousin. She didn't know if she should share this news with Russell. No one in her family liked to talk about Roger Watson especially her.

"Miss Teach?" Russell was staring at Libby.

"Oh sorry. My mind just wandered there for a moment. What were you saying?"

"I wanted to know if you thought I'd be like my dad."

Libby made a quick decision to not let Russell know of their relationship.

"No, you don't have to be like him. You can be whatever kind of person you chose to be."

"I want to be in the Army."

"Then that's what you should focus on. When you feel sad or overwhelmed with life in a detention center, you just think about the day in the not so distant future when you will walk out of here and into the Army."

They continued talking about life in the detention center. By the end of the meeting Libby couldn't decide if she thought Russell was hoping to be like his father or afraid he'd end up on death row like his father.

Chapter 53
Mike

Mike was reading some information on becoming a detective while he waited for Libby in the lobby area. He was ready to get their life as a married couple started. He wanted to take care of her and attempt to keep her out of trouble. Somehow he doubted he would be able to do that. He was scheduled to take the detective's test in a month. He felt confident he would pass and the bump in pay would be a timely bonus. The one drawback would be not having Jump as his partner anymore. Jump had no desire to become a detective or ever leave being a beat cop. He liked patrolling and being close to the people he had sworn to serve and protect. He was good at it too. But lately there had been some tension between the two partners. Mike knew it all went back to that day in the storage shed when they agreed to take the drug money.

They needed that money, more so than the department needed to lock it away in evidence. Jump used it to pay for college for his kids and Mike used his share on the purchase of the house he and Libby picked out together. Libby never questioned how he came up with the money. She assumed he'd been saving for years.

Neither Jump nor Mike ever mentioned the cash to anyone else and they didn't discuss it with each other. It was as if the event never happened. However, now there seemed to be an underlying sense of mistrust between them. A sort of "if they took some money what else were they capable of" mentality. Mike thought it might just be better to part ways after all. He was pondering all of this when Libby entered the waiting area.

"You ready?" She asked.

"I am. Got some good studying done for the exam next month."

"I'm glad you were able to make good use of the time. I hated for you to have to wait out here for me."

"You know I wouldn't have it any other way. How was Russell?"

"He's fine. It'll be an adjustment for him to get used to living behind bars for the next few years. All he seems to want is to be in the Army."

"I'm not sure the Army will take him. Just have to wait and see."

"I'm not going to tell him that. It's the only hope he has for surviving this place."

"Enough about him. How about you and I go somewhere and get a bite to eat and plan our future?"

"That sounds nice. What do you want to talk about?" asked Libby.

"I want to set the date for when you become Mrs. Libby O'Malley."

Libby smiled and grabbed Mike's hand as they made their way out of the facility.

Chapter 54
Russell

After Libby left Russell, he was taken to a large room used for group therapy sessions. He was escorted there but left alone in the room while he waited for others to arrive. Russell walked to a window and happened to see Libby walking in the parking lot with the man he knew was her fiancé. He watched as the two shared a brief kiss before Libby got in the car.

"What cha' looking at retard?" Startled, Russell turned to see who had snuck up on him.

There was a big boy who appeared older by a year or two standing very close to Russell.

"I said what are you looking at, retard?" The older boy had a terrible case of acne along with a couple of missing teeth. He was not handsome by any means and clearly used his size to intimidate others.

"Nothing," said Russell.

"You calling me nothing?" The bully gave Russell a push as he said it.

"I didn't call you anything. Just leave me alone or you'll regret it."

"I ain't afraid of a shrimp like you." He gave Russell another shove.

"You should be. I don't put up with anybody picking on me. So I'm warning you to back off." Russell determined he was not going to be bullied anymore. If it meant hurting someone then he would. Just like he took care of Wayne he could take care of anyone who bothered him from now on.

"Boys, get away from each other and take a seat."
An older man entered the room carrying a pile of papers.
"Harrison, you sit over here." He pointed to a chair near the
door to the room.

"This ain't over, retard." Harrison said under his
breath as his made his way to the designated chair.

"You must be Russell. I'm Fred and I take care of
you guys when you're between sessions. If you need
anything you come to me. How about you sit here by me?"

Russell nodded his agreement and sat down. Soon
other boys filed in the room and Fred made the necessary
introductions. The meeting turned out to be nothing more
than a gripe session and the guys mostly complained about
the food. Russell couldn't wait to be alone.

Later that same week as the young men were
getting showers, Russell was in a stall shampooing his hair.
The curtain was ripped open and Harrison stood there
naked and grinning at Russell. Harrison was twirling a
toothbrush that had the end shaved to a sharp point. It was a
homemade prison shank. Russell knew some of the other
guys made knives and weapons out of everyday items and
now Russell was afraid of what Harrison planned to do to
him with the makeshift knife. Harrison stepped in the
shower and pulled the curtain closed.

"So retard, I need my back washed and I got an itch
you're gonna scratch." Harrison reached out with the
toothbrush and rubbed it along Russell's face.

"Get out of my shower," Russell said.

"Make me, retard," Harrison said as he placed the
toothbrush on the soap dish.

"I'll call for a guard."

"The guards like to leave us alone while we take showers. That way no one can accuse them of being boy lovers."

"HELP!" Russell hoped someone would come and the bigger kid would have to go away. Just then the shower curtain was again opened but there was not a guard. A group of boys were interested in the events unfolding in the stall.

"Hey retard, give us a show," said a stocky youth of about fifteen.

"Yeah, come on. We want to see some love." A group of five young men gathered near the stall and began chanting.

"Do it! Do it!"

The chanting grew louder and Harrison was encouraged by their cheers. He reached for Russell but Russell knocked his hand away.

"Hey that hurt. Now you're really gonna pay."

"No one is ever going to make me do the nasty again."

The other boys laughed at Russell's description of what was about to take place.

"Come on, retard. Give me a kiss." Harrison moved closer to Russell. This was the moment Russell could take no more. He grabbed the makeshift shank and jabbed it into Harrison's eyes. The bully screamed in pain and clutched at his face. Russell continued to jab the toothbrush at any part of Harrison's body Russell could reach. Harrison was screaming in agony.

"Fight! Fight!" The crowd of onlookers changed their taunting words for a romantic tryst to words that encouraged a fight between the boys.

"Come on Harrison, fight back."

"Yeah, don't be such a girl."

The boys continued to taunt Harrison, but he didn't hear them. Harrison was crying in agony. Russell continued to stab anywhere on Harrison he could reach. Eventually Russell managed to ram the toothbrush into Harrison's neck. As he pulled the shank out of Harrison's neck he simply thrust it back in over and over again. Harrison fell to the ground unable to defend himself. The other boys became silent as they watched Harrison's blood run down the shower drain.

"What's going on over here?" One of the two guards asked as he walked over to the crowd of boys.

"You pansies watching a peep show or something?" The other guard looked in the shower and saw Russell covered in blood and holding the toothbrush. Harrison was not moving. "We got a situation," he said to the other guard. "Call for backup."

"Kid you need to hand me that toothbrush." The same guard was calmly talking to Russell and attempting to disarm him. Russell looked at the guard and stretched out his hand for the guard to get the weapon. "That's good. Now you come on out of there and let's get you dried off and then we can talk about what happened." The guard was a seasoned officer and knew he needed to exhibit a peaceful demeanor, so all the boys would follow suit. Russell stepped out of the shower and the other guard placed a towel around Russell.

"I'll stay with this one until help arrives," said the first guard. "You boys break it up. Go on back to your rooms."

He was too late to help Harrison who was lying in a fetal position on the shower floor. The guard reached in and turned off the water and watched, along with the boys, as Russell was led away.

When Russell was walking past the onlookers he saw them staring at him. They seemed to be a little afraid of him now. Russell winked and gave them a grin. Russell decided he liked his new persona. No one would bully him again, ever.

Chapter 55
A Year Later

Over the course of the next several months the killing of Harrison was investigated and determined that Russell was provoked into hurting the older boy and that Russell was ultimately simply defending himself. Since Russell was already in the detention center and receiving counseling, nothing more was to be done. The detention center didn't want any bad publicity, so they only assigned more private sessions for Russell.

Libby received approval from the warden and was able to continue her visits with Russell. At each session she discovered more about Russell and the tragic childhood he endured. She already had enough material for her case study in her course work, but she kept meeting with him in the hope that he would have a positive experience with an adult. Hopefully, he would be able to leave the juvenile detention center at the end of his sentence and enter society with a chance at leading a relatively normal life.

Libby attempted to keep the meetings with Russell focused on positive events in his life such as his work toward getting his GED. She did not inform him of their relationship and as far as she knew Russell never found out any more about his murderous father. When talk of his mother came up she tried to point out the positive things his mother did for him, but she knew Russell resented his mother for her lack of concern about him. Today was Russell's birthday and Libby doubted his mother would visit.

"How are you doing today, Russell?"

"I'm alright. I got an A on my history test."

"That's great. You seem to be doing well with your online courses."

"I like getting to work on my own. I'm ahead of the other guys my age." Russell was proud that he was doing something better than the boys his age at the center.

"Is history still your favorite subject?"

"Yes, it is. I like learning about the French Revolution and how they invented the guillotine," said Russell.

Libby had deep concerns about how much he enjoyed the bloodier aspects of history. He was always telling her some recent fact he learned about methods of torture used by humans over the centuries. "Try to focus on the positive outcomes of these major events. The French were on the road to democracy although it was still a long way off."

"I know that but it's more interesting to read about what they did to anyone who rebelled against them. You know they liked to hold the decapitated head up so everyone could see? And they say some people still blinked too."

"Enough about the beheadings. Do you realize what today is?"

"Yeah, but I don't think about it much."

"Everyone needs to celebrate their birthdays."

"Why? It's just another day and it's never been special for me anyway."

"Has your mom been to see you?"

"I got a letter from her. She says she's too busy at Sassy A. Ever since Lucky Sam was sent to prison she's been running the place. She says she can't get away." Russell looked down at his feet as he said this. Libby knew it bothered Russell that his own mother never took the time to come and visit him.

"Did she send you a gift?"

"She put a five-dollar bill in the letter and the warden added it to my spending account."

"That was nice of her," Libby said.

"If you say so. But I know the money just makes her feel better about not coming to see me. It's been over a year since I saw her."

Libby was somewhat amazed at Russell's insight to his mother's gift. The woman could surely take a day off to visit her son. Libby may just be a graduate student learning about behavioral issues, but she did recognize the influence a mother could have over her child. Especially a single mother and a son. Plenty of notorious criminals, and serial killers in particular, had very poor and abusive relationships with their mothers. If Russell did not get proper psychiatric treatment, there is no telling what his future might hold. Examining the backgrounds of known criminals who grew up in similar situations to Russell, the outlook did not look very promising for him.

Libby remembered reading about one famous killer whose mother was a teenager when she got pregnant. This was during a time in history where girls were frowned upon and deemed loose and immoral for their promiscuity if they ended up pregnant. To avoid any negative comments from the community the girl was sent to live with an out-of-town relative and when she came back with a baby boy it was explained that he was her little brother. The poor boy was raised by his grandparents even though the mother was around. He never felt like he belonged and when he was an adult he went on a murderous killing spree. He left a trail of over thirty women whose bodies he discarded in wooded areas as if they were simply trash. Ultimately, he was executed. Libby did not want Russell to have a future like that. One killer in the family tree was enough.

Libby had made Russell her secret project. She was going to keep visiting him until he was released. Mike wondered why she spent so much time with Russell. Just that morning they had gotten into an argument about her frequent trips to the detention center.

"You really need to stop going out there. Every time you come back you seem depressed," Mike said over their morning coffee.

"I feel sorry for him. He has no one who cares. His mother is too busy with her own life to even visit him."

"He's still not your responsibility but you are mine. Now that you're expecting I want you to be careful. I don't like you going out there and who knows what your mood swings are doing to the baby."

"Mike, that is a ridiculous statement. Women have been having mood swings and caring about other people for centuries. Don't go all macho policeman on me. I will keep seeing Russell and if you say no I'll just go more." Libby got up from the breakfast table and began cleaning up the dishes.

"Oh my gosh, Libby. You are so stubborn." Mike grabbed his car keys and strapped on his gun and left the house.

"Well, goodbye to you too." Libby had tears in her eyes. They'd been married a year and now she was a few weeks pregnant. This was supposed to be the most exciting time of their lives and he was being a jerk about it. Libby went to the closet and got the gift she had for Russell and headed out the door to go to the detention center.

Getting back to her discussion with Russell, Libby asked him if he had friends who knew today was his birthday.

"I don't have any friend here and I don't want any. When I get out of here I'm not gonna hang out with any of them so why make friends?"

"Humans need social interaction with each other. It's OK to have a few friends while you're here," Libby said.

"Nope. I don't want any friends. Besides, I've got you. You're the only person who cares about me."

"Russell, I do care about you and that's why I am telling you it is OK to make some friends. It'll make the time here go much faster."

"Well, maybe." Russell only said that to make Libby happy.

"I do have something for you." Libby reached to the floor and pulled out the gift bag she tried to keep hidden from Russell. The gift had already been checked out by the officers on duty and they agreed to leave it in the bag if Libby brought the bag back out with her.

"Gee thanks. I didn't expect anything." Russell reached into the bag and pulled out a thick book about American involvement in every war since the days before she was a country. "This is great." Russell began looking through the book.

"There's a chapter on the history of the earliest Army Rangers. I thought you would enjoy reading about that since you love the Army so much."

"Yes, I do and thanks. I'll probably have it all read by the next time you come to see me."

Libby chuckled and said, "I believe you will."

They continued talking a little longer and then Libby collected her things and told Russell goodbye.

Chapter 56
Russell

Russell continued to do well in his studies and read the birthday book within the first week. He did not take Libby's advice on making friends. In fact, he had gained a reputation of being a scrappy fighter and although most of the other boys left him alone there was always a newcomer who tried to pick a fight with him. They saw the smaller Russell as someone to be intimated and an easy mark. The newbies, as they were called by the other boys, felt they needed to assert their dominance and beating up Russell seemed like the way to do it.

One night as Russell was brushing his teeth, he leaned over to get some water to rinse out his mouth. A newbie walked by and roughly shoved Russell's head down into the sink. The action cause Russell to gash his eyebrow on the faucet causing a deep cut.

"Aw the puny boy's got a boo-boo," said the taller boy whose name was Brad but all the kids called him Tank because he was built like one.

"You shouldn't have done that," Russell said as he dabbed at the cut over his eye with his washcloth.

"I'm not afraid of no skinny rat like you. I was on the football team and I can bench-press more weight than you." Tank had been in one too many fights at school and even though he was a star athlete the coaches couldn't step in and save him anymore. The last fight had ended up with the other guy going to the emergency room with a broken collar bone, broken rib, and a concussion, and needing thirty-seven stitches. The parents of that boy wanted the football star gone. The school district had to expel him and he was charged with assault. The judge looked at his record and told him it was time he learned a lesson and the juvenile detention center was the place for him. Gone were his dreams of football fame and now Tank carried his rage with him. He was ready to unleash his pent-up anger on someone and Russell seemed like the perfect patsy.

"I'm only going to tell you once. Go away," said Russell.

"Or what? Puny boy will cry for his momma?"

"No, you'll be crying for your momma. That is, if I decide to let you live."

"Hah! You're a funny kid. Like I said, I ain't afraid o' no little punk like you," said the bigger boy as he gave Russell a shove. The push was firm enough that he caused Russell to stumble backward slipping on the wet floor and tripping into the sink. This angered Russell. By now some of the other boys in the bathroom had seen the commotion and wandered over to watch. They knew Russell may look small but he was incredibly strong and Tank was about to find out his mistake in thinking he could intimidate Russell.

"Come on punk. Let's see if you're man enough to take me on," said Tank.

Russell calmly placed his bloodied cloth in the sink and stepped up to Tank. If Russell were taller they would have been face to face but Tank towered over Russell and laughed at his attempt at intimidation. The crowd knew this was just Russell's way of getting the other boy to initiate the fight which kept Russell from getting into any more trouble.

Tank fell for the tactic and picked up Russell and threw him down on the floor momentarily knocking the wind out of him. He scrambled up and then charged at

Tank and began using his fists and legs to clobber Tank. The attack caught the bigger kid off guard and Russell had the advantage. He pushed Tank against the sink and as Tank turned to get away Russell used that moment to grab Tank's head and slam it into the mirror over the sink repeatedly hitting his face into it causing it to crack. By now the onlookers had grown noisy in their desire to see a fight. Guards ran in and removed the two combatants.

Tank was taken to the infirmary and his faced received thirteen stitches. He was more upset with the number of stitches they put in than he was with the fact he would have a scar running down his cheek. Russell explained how the older boy started the fight and they could ask anyone and they'd tell them the same. Russell also had to get the gash over his eye stitched-up, but he only needed three. His scar would blend into his eyebrow and therefore not mar his face permanently. He did have a black eye but that would heal and it served as a temporary reminder to the other guys in the detention center to leave him alone. Word spread fast about the fight and Russell's reputation as a tough fighter grew.

Russell was in the library working on his school work. Some of the kids in there were pointing at him and whispering. He didn't care. He knew they'd leave him alone and no one would come sit beside him either. That was fine with him because it meant no one would be looking over his shoulder and trying to see what he was researching. He knew his dad's name was Roger Watson and he had been executed a long time ago, but Russell wondered if he had any family on his dad's side. Who knew? Maybe he was the heir to a fortune or something.

Silent Rage

He entered the name into the Internet search engine the students were allowed to use. He got several hits. A bunch really. Evidently Roger Watson was a common name.

One guy was an accountant and he was black. That wasn't his dad. Another guy was a musician at some college. He was still alive so that couldn't be any relation. Russell kept reading about all these men who were definitely not his father. Finally, Russell added the word killer and was able to get some results about his father. He read many news reports about the Trailer Park Murderer. He read about the victims and their families. Eventually he came across a short article that included a picture of Roger's family. In the picture was a woman the caption said was his mother and another woman that was his sister. There was a young girl with this woman. He read the caption and sat back in shock. He read it again, "the killer's family refrained from any comments on his crime. Pictured are his mother, Gail Watson, his sister Francis Teach, and his niece, Libby Teach."

Russell wondered if it was the same Libby Teach. How many people from around here could be named Libby Teach. He searched Libby's name. Again, there were numerous hits. Her social media sites, her wedding photo, and a few high school pictures. He looked closely and thought they resembled his Libby Teach. He didn't know what to think about it. If he was related to Libby, then it made his feelings for her wrong. He secretly loved her, almost like the kind of mother he wished he had but also in a way like he wanted to live with her forever and take care of her. He needed to think about this new turn of events. He was also a little angry at her for never telling him. She knew the day she read the paper telling her who his real father was. He couldn't wait for their next visit.

Russell was in the conference room waiting for Libby to show up. He knew she sometimes ran late because her four-month-old twin girls demanded so much of her time. He tried not to resent them for taking Libby away from him, but he did anyway. He liked that she let him call her Libby now. Sometimes it was hard to not call her Ms. Teach even though she was really Mrs. O'Malley. Since they were really related he should've been calling her Libby all along. He might be upset with her for not telling him they were related but he was also glad she still made time for him. His mother didn't even send any money this year on his birthday. Libby brought him another book and some chocolate candy.

"Hi Russell," Libby entered the room and greeted him.

"Hi."

She walked over to the table and put her belongings on it. Looking at Russell's black eye and stitches she asked, "What happened?"

"Nothing, just an accident in the bathroom."

"Russell, how many times have I come and you've had some sort of injury and they all seem to come in the bathroom? I'm not blind I can tell you've been fighting. Are you hurt anywhere else?"

"No. It's really ok. Just a new kid bumping into me."

"Do I need to speak with the warden?"

"No. That'd only make me look like a baby. I can handle this. I've only got a couple more years anyway."

"If it keeps on I will step in and say something whether or not you want me to."

"I can take care of myself. I always have."

"We'll see. So on another topic, how is your school work coming? Last time I was here you were working on an essay."

"Yeah, I got a B on it. I don't like to write. I would rather just tell someone what I know. Maybe I'd like to be a reporter and, you know, uncover the truth about things." Russell wanted to ask her about Roger Watson and their relationship.

"You could be a reporter, but you'd have to write about the news. Maybe you could cover news when the US is involved in any wars."

"Maybe. Or maybe I could cover crime. Since you know my dad was a killer maybe I could investigate who they were before they killed or who their family was. If their family even cared about them or not."

"Why this sudden interest in reporting? I thought you only cared about joining the Army?"

"I've been researching who my dad was and if he had any family or anybody who cared about him. I thought maybe he was like me and had no one or maybe he came from a rich family and I'm the only heir to a fortune."

"I'm not sure delving into your dad's history is such a good thing for you to do."

"Why is that? Is it because you're related to him too?"

Libby gasped and stared at Russell. "What makes you think I am related to him?"

Russell reached into his pocket and pulled out a folded piece of computer paper. Printed on it was a copy of the photo and the description naming Roger's family including his niece, Libby. He handed the paper to Libby. "This is why I think you're related. Which also makes you related to me."

Libby took the paper and unfolded it. She read the caption and looked at the picture.

"I didn't know there were any pictures of me like this."

"So it's you, isn't it?"

"Yes."

"Why didn't you tell me you knew who my dad was? What are we cousins or something?"

"Yes we are and the reason I didn't tell you was because I didn't think it would help you. You had enough going on in your life to think about other family members."

"I had no one who cared. My own mother doesn't come and visit. Why wouldn't you think it would help me to have someone who cared. Do you care?" Russell was getting irritated and his voice was rising in anger. A guard looked their way.

Libby nodded they were OK. "I'm sorry. I do care and that's why I come to visit you."

"But you lied."

"I didn't lie. I just didn't tell you. I guess I don't really have a good reason. It just seemed like the right thing to do at the time."

"Well, I can just keep on taking care of myself like I always have. I don't need anyone which means I don't need you."

"Now Russell, we've talked about the need for a support system when you leave. I want to make sure you can transition back into society when that day comes."

"I'll do it by myself. I think it would be better if you didn't come anymore."

"You're not serious."

"I am. Goodbye, cousin Libby." Russell left the room. Libby sat for a moment thinking about the relationship Russell had unearthed in his research. Libby was truly concerned for Russell's future now. He had no one to help him. She feared he was turning into someone who had no regard for the feelings of others. She feared he was turning into his dad.

Enjoy the following preview of *Deafening Rage* coming soon!

Chapter 1 Russell

The heat hit him right in the face as Russell Thomas exited the gates of The Bluffton Regional Youth Center, or The Brick as locals called it. He saw the shadow of a woman standing at the end of the sidewalk and assumed it must be his mother since the warden told him she'd be the one getting him. He had not seen her since the day he was locked up for murder over five years ago. It surprised him she bothered to come.

"Hey mom," he said. The little boy inside of him put a smile on his face at the sight of her. He hoped they could start fresh and be a real family like a mother and son should be.

"Take the keys to this truck and this cash. Drive somewhere far way and don't come back." She frowned as she spoke. "I am not interested in playing mommy to a killer. I want you to move on and stay out of my life." Loretta Thomas didn't share any hugs with her only child. She didn't even smile at him. Instead she handed him the envelope containing some money and the keys to the vehicle then turned and walked away.

Russell took the items from her and watched as she headed over to a late model SUV and opened the door on the passenger side and got in. He couldn't tell who the driver was, but he wished he was the one leaving with his mother. He followed the car's progress as it left the parking lot. Loretta didn't bother to wave goodbye.

"Happy birthday to me," Russell mumbled. A small part of him died at that moment. There was no longer any hope of belonging anywhere, no family to go home to, no one to care about him. What a way to spend a birthday. But he wasn't really surprised. It wasn't like his mother had bothered celebrating any of his previous birthdays. *Eighteen years old and I can't even drive.* Russell was sinking into despair.

"You gonna stand there all day?"

Russell startled out of his musings and turned to look at the burly officer walking toward him.

"I don't really know what to do," said Russell.

"That's easy. You get in a car and put as much distance between this place and you as you can and then you start a new life." He didn't say this with any form of malice. The guard, everyone called Spook, was one of the nicer officers at The Brick.

"My mom just gave me the keys to a truck."

"So, what's your hold-up?" Spook continued walking toward the parking lot. It was shift change, he was eager to get home and relax.

"I don't know how to drive." Russell's comment caused the guard to stop and turn back. He stood there and gave a penetrating stare at Russell. It was unnerving Russell until Spook finally spoke.

"Driver's ed is something we don't offer here. But I got an idea," he said. "I got a buddy who runs the marina over on Elena's Point and he always needs extra hands for odd jobs. I'll get another officer and together we'll drive you to the place. After that you're on your own."

"I'd appreciate that."

"Sit on that bench over there and I'll be back in a sec."

It'd been almost ten years since that day. Russell learned how to survive and how not to depend on anyone. It seemed people always let him down eventually, anyway.

His string of girlfriends was proof of that. He looked at them all now. Each one curled up inside a blanket made of earth. Some had been there longer than others. He raised his hand to the gleam of moonlight and looked at the lock of hair he held and watched as it danced between his fingers. It once resided on the head of a girl named Amy May, now it would be part of Russell's macabre collection. He hated that Amy let him down. He had hoped she would be the one who would take away all the loneliness. *Bet she wishes that too, now.*

For more information on the second book in the rage series go to https://defunk.net/.

Author's Bio

"What trouble did you get into today?" is a question often asked by DE Funk's husband. While he says this a bit tongue in cheek, it is not without merit. DE believes in experiencing rather than watching as well asking rather than wondering. An active person who loves everything from golfing to biking to walking, DE Funk has traveled around the world but calls the South home. Having worn the hats of teacher and college instructor of history and criminal justice, DE Funk uses her years of learning to write crime fiction. *Silent Rage* is her debut novel and *Deafening Rage* will be released very soon. DE is married and has three children. Visit her website at https://defunk.net/.

You can show your appreciation by leaving a review on Amazon, Barnes and Noble or the Kobo store. If you write a review, please be sure to email DE Funk at diane@defunk.net so that she can express gratitude.